I0607823

PSYCHIC LINK

KATE ALLENTON

Copyright © 2016 Coastal Escape Publishing,
LLC

All rights reserved.

ISBN-10: 1-944237-29-1
ISBN-13: 978-1-944237-29-5

The unauthorized reproduction or distribution of this copyrighted work is illegal. Criminal copyright infringement (including infringement without monetary gain) is investigated by the FBI and is punishable by up to 5 years in federal prison and a fine of $250,000.

Please purchase only authorize electronic editions and do not participate in, or encourage, the electronic piracy of Copyrighted materials. Your support of the author's rights is appreciated.

This book is a work of fiction. Names, character, places, and incidents are the products of the author's imagination or use fictitiously. Any resemblance to actual events, locals or persons, living or dead, is entirely coincidental.

All rights reserved. Except for use in any review, the reproduction or utilization of this work, in whole or in part, in any form by any electronic, mechanical or other means now known or hereafter invented, is forbidden without the written permission of the publisher.

Published by Coastal Escape Publishing

Discover other titles by Kate Allenton

www.kateallenton.com

Chapter 1

Cara crossed her legs and let her gaze sweep over the man standing in her doorway. He looked in need of a good tumble in the dryer and a few eye drops to clear the redness from his eyes. Stubble covered the sexiest jaw she'd ever seen. Broad shoulders and muscular thighs gave him that bad-boy vibe that screamed ride me all night long. Damn, now that song would play in her head the rest of the day.

His Caribbean blue eyes were mesmerizing. His brown hair matched the icing on the brownie sitting on her desk. He'd make pretty babies. All she'd need was his sperm. Would he be offended if she handed him a cup and lifted her shirt to help him along?

"Are you Cara Thatcher?" His voice was deceptively calm, his gaze assessing. Muscles coiled in his arms, his jaw clenched, and Cara had this gut-wrenching feeling that if she answered his simple question, her life would be forever changed.

"Who's asking?" she deflected and rose from her chair, ready to fire whatever security guard he'd slipped past downstairs. People called the workers at Linked Inc. quacks for having abilities. They weren't the crazy ones. Crazy people were unpredictable, and...this guy, although good looking, might very well be tiptoeing the line.

His jaw ticked as he slipped his hand into his pocket. Cara kept her finger hovering over the alarm button beneath her desk. The scent of baby powder drifted to her nose, making her pause. The sweet, innocent scent was so at odds with his appearance.

The stranger's blue eyes darkened while zeroing in on her fingers, and he slowly pulled his wallet free with two fingers as if he were a criminal trying to calm a trigger-happy police officer. "Relax, lady."

Relax wasn't in Cara's vocabulary, even if he looked like a sleep-deprived, crazed daddy in need of a night off.

He opened his wallet and held out his badge. FBI? She plopped back down in her chair. The tension in her shoulders deflated, like the air in her tires the last time they'd been slashed. That crazy person had never been caught. Cara's cheeks heated under his stare. Overreact much? Gah..."How can I help you, Agent..."

"Special Agent Cooper Cruz." He gestured to the seat, asking permission to sit.

Cruz? The only Cruz she knew was Eric. The one that she'd dated. The same one who had destroyed her heart by stomping it into a million little pieces. That Cruz was the reason she no longer dated cops. And, although that Cruz and this one didn't look remotely related, she couldn't help the gut punch from having to relive the brief memories. Cara shoved the distant memories away and focused on the man she'd be addressing by his first name, in an effort to disassociate the two. It was the least she could do.

"Yes, of course. Please have a seat, Agent. Is it okay if I call you Cooper?"

Cara opened her desk drawer, pulled out her phone, and turned on the recorder. It was standard practice that she recorded everything so the authorities and her clients could review the message from a spirit or her visions later when they weren't so emotional. It didn't hurt that it protected her ass from lawsuits. "You don't mind if I record, do you? I like to make sure you guys don't misinterpret whatever it is I say."

"Uh, sure."

Silently she ran through her work calendar in her mind. She hadn't had an appointment scheduled with Agent Cruz. She would have remembered. She would have canceled or pushed him off on one of her other sisters, just because of his last name. She smiled smoothly, betraying nothing of her annoyance. Her mother would be proud.

"Thanks, and sure, you can call me Coop." He sat across from her, and his gaze traveled over the contents of her office. His expression darkened with an unreadable emotion as he crossed and uncrossed his arms. He looked one step away from bolting out the door, until his gaze landed on the "unofficial" certificate the FBI had given her for helping to pinpoint clues that led to the apprehension of a serial killer. He lifted a brow. "So it's true? You helped catch the notorious Tri-County Reaper."

The Tri-County Reaper was a serial killer of the worst kind. He was smart.

He'd been terrorizing Florida, Alabama, and Georgia cops for ten years, disposing of his victims' bodies inside the fresh graves of people just laid to rest. It was the last place any cop would look, and the only place where he'd left the evidence behind that had sent him away for life.

"I don't catch criminals, Agent....Coop. I merely provide new clues for the police to investigate."

He nodded and ran his hand through his already disheveled hair. "You come highly recommended."

Doubt that. Feed me another line. Her brow rose instantly. Her help was usually swept under the rug. Her involvement was usually the last resort, after all the leads had turned cold. Who did this guy think he was kidding?

"I only deal with missing persons or homicides. Which one are you here for?"

Coop's brows dipped. The energy around his aura sparked out like a live wire. His emotions seemed to be bouncing off the walls, even though he remained tight-lipped.

I can't read your mind, buddy. The words were on the tip of her tongue. She could have eased him into a false sense of security, but why bother? He might as well get a first-hand look at crazy if he was asking for a one-way ticket on her crazy train.

"Hopefully, just a missing person."

His answered piqued her interest. She hadn't had a good case in a month.

"Although I'm really here about your other 'ability,'" he said making air quotations with his fingers, as if her ability was as imaginary as unicorns, the tooth fairy, and the unopened bottle of scotch in her desk drawer. She'd been tempted to offer him a shot to loosen his lips. At the rate he was talking, he'd eventually get to his problem by the end of next week.

"My other ability?" she asked, and her interest went from piqued to guarded quicker than a kid being released the last day of school before summer break. She had other abilities, but only a few select friends and family members knew what they entailed. This guy didn't qualify as either. Someone was getting a voodoo doll commissioned in their honor. Cara clicked off the recorder.

"Yeah, you know. The one where you touch people or things and get flashes of their life."

She knew, but how did he? Her affable smile from minutes ago slipped as she pegged him with her gaze. "Who did you say recommended me?"

"Eric Cruz, my brother. Well, technically, he's my half-brother. His mom, my dad…"

"Um...." Cara pressed her lips together, biting back the words she wanted to say. Fuck you, get out of my office, and tell that sorry sack of shit, asshole-from-hell brother of yours to take a flying leap...were just a few. Her clasped fingers turned white as she tried to contain the anger bubbling inside that was on the verge of breaking free. Most days she was a professional, but that name had her sprouting imaginary horns. She should send him packing. Would a kick in the ass, to pass along to his brother, be unladylike? "I'm sorry. I can't help you."

"He said you'd say that. He actually said you'd say a lot worse, and told me not to bother, but I'm desperate. We're desperate." His wild blue eyes searched hers. "Please, don't turn me away because of what Eric did."

Cara held up her hand and rose from the chair. Any more mention of that name and he was getting a first-rate show. Stuff would be thrown; hexes would be made, and she would personally toss his ass out of her office...from the window. Screw trying to maintain an adult demeanor. Her shrink would charge overtime, and she'd need bail money, but it would be worth it.

"I'm sorry. I can't help you. Maybe you should find someone else, a little less familiar." Her voice was firm and final.

He'd already ripped the Band-Aid off the wound. No way in hell would she wait around to see what was next. Childish, probably; unprofessional, absolutely, but it didn't matter. Unless called by the President himself, or her mother dragging Cara by the ear, she wouldn't be helping anyone with Eric's DNA. It was a scientific fact that traits were passed around. She wasn't chancing that Eric had received all the shitty ones.

Cara crossed her arms over her chest, for his protection, and to prevent her ass from having to spend a night behind bars. She rounded the desk and moved to the door.

"He said that you'd say that too." Cooper walked to the door and held out his hand. "It was nice meeting you."

Cara glanced down at his outstretched hand and shook her head. If Eric had told him about her ability, then this *special agent* must be thinking he was smarter than the average badge. With a single touch, she'd know everything about whatever he was working on, regardless of whether she'd wanted to or not. She may be blonde, but that sun-kissed shade came straight from a box.

Cooper's lips twitched as he dropped his hand. Her reaction seemed to amuse him. "It was worth a shot."

"Nice try, Agent." Cara pursed her lips together. Bastard.

She watched him as he left the office and stood in front of the elevator. She was making sure he got inside.

"He's a hottie. Who is he? Is he in the running as a baby daddy donor?" Cara's sister, Harper, asked as she approached. Her model figure and porcelain skin turned the detectives into dogs in heat just by being in her presence. With Harper's beautiful looks, and the calming gift she had, Cara and the others only brought her in on special assignments. Cooper might have had better luck with her.

"No one," Cara said loud enough for Cooper to hear as she held his gaze one last time before he stepped onto the elevator. He frowned.

"Look at that pitiful face and tell me the truth. Did you show him your boobs and then tell him he couldn't play?"

He should be so lucky. Cara, on the other hand, wouldn't be. One touch and she'd know all of his dirty secrets, just like how she'd discovered Eric was screwing her best friend. One simple brush of his shoulder, and it was as if she was a voyeur watching the man whore and his skank getting busy in her bed. She'd tossed his ass out and burnt a perfectly good bed, not to mention some of his "personal" items. He'd never miss them.

"I told him I couldn't help him." Cara walked back into her office. Harper leaned against the doorframe.

"Why not? He's a cop, right? If it's in an official capacity, we normally don't turn them away."

True as that statement was, it didn't change a thing. Cara snagged the brownie from her desk and took a bite, savoring the chocolate as she chewed. It was either that or the booze in her drawer. Hell, it might take both. "His last name is Cruz."

Harper's luminous eyes widened in astonishment before they flickered in amusement. Cara could count on her sisters to enjoy watching her squirm. "Is he related?"

Cara nodded, not bothering for a verbal answer as she shoved another bite of chocolate-y goodness into her mouth.

"Ohhhh...well then. I guess that says enough because you know....the sins of the brother and all that." She turned to leave and grabbed the door to shut it behind her. "You know...if that were the case, then we'd be responsible for every single one of Quinn's actions too."

Low blow. Cara's mouth parted as she narrowed her eyes. It was one thing for Quinn to be crazy, another for someone to blame Cara. Her sister, Quinn, was the poster child of crazy town.

The brownie Cara had been enjoying suddenly tasted like sawdust as she swallowed around the lump lodged in her throat. Damn her. Harper quickly shut the door as the remainder of Cara's brownie sailed through the air. It splattered against the door.

"See what you made me do?" A perfectly good brownie, ruined.

Harper peeked inside. "Don't forget you drew the short straw and have to help Aunt Betty at the bar tonight."

If Cara had another brownie, that one would be splattered along with the first. If Quinn was the poster child of crazy town, Aunt Betty was the founder.

Harper's laughter carried past the office window, where she wiggled her fingers goodbye.

It wasn't as though Cara was being irrational. It made perfect sense. Eric was a low-life, bottom-dwelling, scum sucker. It stood to reason the other Cruz would be too. DNA, damn it. Why couldn't everyone else see the connection? Maybe if he hadn't said, "*We* need your help," she would have listened. She shook her head, probably not even then. Cara stomped over to the splattered brownie and started cleaning up the pieces, much like she'd done with her life after Eric.

Cara tossed the brownie into the trashcan, moved over to her window, and glanced out at the calming view. The crystal blue water of the ocean gleamed in the distance, lowering her blood pressure. The only thing better would be to hear the crashing waves. She made a mental note to take her recorder next time she went to the beach.

She'd expected to see tourists walking by on the street below, with shining bright sunburns, while wearing big straw hats and bikinis. Instead, she found Harper standing outside the building doors deep in conversation with the *other* Cruz.

The anger that had been simmering in her gut started to boil. The Thornton clan was about to be minus one sister at Sunday dinner. Mom could always conceive another.

Harper tapped Coop's arm, pointed to Cara's window, and waved. Damn her. Damn him.

Chapter 2

Cara pulled up outside The Blue Bar and parked between two unmarked patrol cars. Fluorescent blue neon lights flashed the name as two scantily clad women disappeared inside. The badge bunnies were out in full force for mating season.

"Are you there yet?" Cara's sister, Quinn, asked into the Bluetooth protruding from Cara's ear.

"Yeah, I just pulled up outside the bar. How come I'm always the one stuck dealing with Aunt Betty?" Cara knew the answer without Quinn saying a word. Cara was the responsible sister.

"Quit bitching and take one for the team. You know, if I was stateside, I'd handle it myself."

Cara smiled at Quinn's response, even though they both knew she was full of crap. "No, you wouldn't."

"Fine, but I would have paid one of our other sisters to do it."

"True." Cara bobbed her head as if weighing her sister's answer. Quinn marched to her own tune. One that only she could hear, just like the opera-singing Scottish ghost that had haunted her butt last year. She so deserved it.

"I hope you're keeping score. I want brownies for this one, and I'm not talking about the prepackaged crap. I want Mavis' brownies." Mavis was the Scottish cook in Quinn and Collin's castle. Quinn used the bribe often, and Cara wasn't one to ever tell her no. Not when homemade brownies were used as an enticement. Cara grabbed her purse and stepped out of the car. She amended her early demands. "Overnighted. I'm not waiting until Christmas time."

"Deal." Cara was a second from clicking the Bluetooth button to cut her sister off when Quinn added, "I'll do one better."

"Yeah? How can you do better than Mavis' brownies overnighted from Scotland? Are you sending Mavis too?"

Cara asked and adjusted the shirt of her uniform to cover her black bra poking out from the top.

"Not Mavis, but close. Ian's already in route with a fresh batch, and he's going to need a place to crash while in town. I told him you had room. Love you, bye." Quinn quickly disconnected the call.

Ian. Just what Cara needed. Of course, Quinn would saddle Cara with a horny Highlander, with roaming hands, after a night of fighting off advances from drunk cops. Cara tilted her head back and forth to ease the coiled tension in her neck. Her day was getting better by the minute. What next?

I've got this. Cara adjusted the hem of her uniform. The blue schoolgirl skirt barely covered her ass, and her white cotton top was cut into a V at the top and molded to the curves of her generous round breasts. She was a walking felony. She headed into the bar to fulfill her family duty. Music blared from the speakers as women danced and men crowded the stage. Cara had been promised a slow night working behind the bar, but this... Cara shook her head as she headed toward Aunt Betty behind the bar.

"You're late, sugar," Aunt Betty called out and lifted the bar top so Cara could get behind it.

"And you lied, Aunt Betty. You promised me a slow night," she said, trying to bite back her annoyance.

"This is slow," Betty argued, pulling a beer from the cooler. She handed it to one of the guy's perched on the barstool. He wobbled. Cara registered the rest of the men sitting nearby, DUI, DUI, crossdresser? She did a double take.

"The girls will be off the stage in thirty minutes, and some of the crowd will leave."

Cara rested her elbows on the bar and scanned the room. The women on the stage were prancing around in strings that barely covered their assets while men stuck money between their fake breasts. Cara shook her head. In another ten minutes, Aunt Betty would probably be on stage. It was a wonder she'd lasted in the FBI as long as she had. Cara bet they'd thrown one hell of a retirement party.

"Did you have your appointment?" Aunt Betty asked.

"Yeah."

"How are your eggs? Are they all scrambled?"

Cara smiled at her question. Aunt Betty was always blunt and blurted out her thoughts. "They're healthy and frozen."

"Good to hear it." Aunt Betty gestured toward the dance floor. "I still think you should conceive the old-fashioned way. With a nice guy, in love, in the bar stockroom, but...do what you must. Tonight's candidates are ripe for the picking. You sure I can't change your mind?"

Aunt Betty elbowed Cara. Her aunt was a feisty old broad who weekly dyed her hair a different color. This week it matched the bright blue of her neon sign.

"I think I'll pass." Cara smiled sweetly at her aunt. She might not have put drunken cops under the *hell no* on her donor list, but she'd rectify that when she got home, right after she added anyone with Cruz as their last name.

"What about Juan, here," Aunt Betty said while smacking the bar-back's ass as he carried a crate of beer mugs. "He's got a fine ass."

"I'm sure his boyfriend, Michal, would agree. Although I'm not sure he'd approve."

"That's not true, Cara." Juan grinned. "We could both be your baby's daddy. Double the pleasure."

"Sorry, Juan. I'm not looking for a daddy. I'm looking for sperm."

"So am I, honey. So am I." Juan high-fived Cara as he passed.

"You keep being picky; your clock isn't just going to quit ticking. It's going to fall out of your uterus onto your yoga mat."

Yoga mat? "Now I know you're mental. You have me confused with Becca. When I get into yoga pants, it's because I opened a five-gallon carton of ice cream."

Cara's sister, Becca, was a nature child. She loved everything organic, including stretching her body into a pretzel. She'd make some guy happy one day.

"Enough chitchat. You know the drill. You've got the far end of the bar, and I'll take the orders from the waitresses."

Cara did know the drill. Betty had taught her nieces at an early age how to mix drinks while Betty was still in the bureau. If she hadn't been the law, they would have arrested her for child endangerment.

Two hours later, Cara was still batting down advances quicker than melting ice cream on a Florida beach, when Aunt Betty disappeared through the back door and returned carrying a diaper bag covered with cute farm animals.

Talk about toppings before the ice cream scoops. "Isn't it a little early to give me a diaper bag?"

"It's not for you, and the one I buy wouldn't ever be as bland as this one."

Cara smiled at the thought. The one Aunt Betty gave her would probably have flashing breasts acting as a bottle from which the baby could feed.

"I can handle the bar by myself for the rest of the night, but would you make like a call girl and make a house call?"

Laughter erupted from Cara's lips. "It's the outfit, isn't it? It screams streetwalker. You should really think about classing the joint up."

"Sex sells, doll. I need this dropped off at a friend's house on the way home."

"Sure." Cara slipped the diaper bag over her shoulder and watched as an approaching man's eyes widened. The color drained from his face as he slowly backtracked away, making Cara's smile widen. The diaper bag worked like man-whore repellant. She should have had this bag slung across her body all night. "What's the address?"

Aunt Betty grabbed a napkin and wrote down the address. "It's an old Victorian house. You can't miss it."

Cara parked on the road in front of an old two-story house. One car was parked in the driveway. Light seeped through the small opening in the closed curtains covering the living room window. The upstairs part of the two-story house was dark. Creepy places like this scared most people, but to her, it was history, and whatever ghosts were haunting the place were normally friendlier than the owner. She slipped out of her car and pulled at the hem of her skirt. Heat seared her cheeks from embarrassment. She should have gone home and changed first. Cara shoved the thoughts aside. Who cared. She'd never be seeing these people again, and they had to know she was coming from Aunt Betty's bar. That alone would explain everything. Cara slipped the strap of the bag over her head as she walked up the drive.

The front door flew open, stopping her in her tracks. A woman emerged from inside the house. Her scream pierced the hot night air. The color of her face was whiter than Cara's ass cheeks. The woman ran down the street, flailing her arms like a teen chasing her favorite band. Who taught that girl how to run? Cara's fingers tensed around the bag's strap as she slowly approached, ready to flee if a knife-wielding maniac should appear. She knew better than to go rushing inside. Momma hadn't raised the dumb chick in a horror flick. Uh-uh, not this girl.

Cara peeked inside the open door and froze. A baby was floating in mid-air. Normally, people wouldn't be able to see the ghost that was holding it, or the other three ghostly presences in the room. Cara wasn't normal. No wonder the chick had run off. To her, the baby probably looked possessed.

Cara shook her head as she walked to the open door. A man stood with his back to her, jumping to try and grab the baby as it was lifted out of his reach. Poor guy.

Cara stepped inside. "Put that baby down, or so help me, I'll have this house blessed and salted to drive your asses out and prevent you all from ever coming back."

All of the ghostly eyes turned toward her, as did the man. Cooper Cruz. The last man on Earth she'd ever thought to see again. Cooper's gaze travelled down her body before meeting her gaze. He spun back to the baby as the baby was lowered to the blanket.

He was quick to grab the baby and cradle it against his chest. "What was that?"

"Strong, mischievous ghosts. I'm sure it takes a lot of energy to move things, and I can only imagine the energy it took to play a game of Keep Away." She walked into the house and shut the door. "You should think about tossing their asses out."

The living room was a mess. Toys were strewn across the floor. Blankets and empty bottles lay nearby. The baby had a T-shirt around his bottom, knotted at the stomach and being held by rubber bands.

A spit-up stain traveled the length of Cooper's shirt in the back.

Laughter burst from her lips, warming her body from the inside out. This explained the walking zombie look from her office.

Cooper glared. She tried to stifle her laugh. Really she did.

"Bad night?" she asked, clearing her throat to hide the humor.

Cooper sighed and kissed the blond peach fuzz on the baby's head. "The worst."

Cara strolled across the room and took the baby from his hands, suppressing the baby's images that formed from the touch.

The scent of baby poop lingered in the air, and it was a toss-up if the stink was coming from the baby or Cooper. "I've got him. Go take a shower and get cleaned up. You both smell like sour milk."

Without a word, Cooper disappeared up the stairs. Cara grabbed one of the blankets and walked into the kitchen, hoping Aunt Betty had thought enough to pack some baby shampoo, among other things she'd need to make everything right. As if that was possible. She was in a Cruz house, and here she was helping. She must be slowly losing her mind. Cara glanced down at the beautiful baby. Had it been just Cooper, she would have walked away, but this sweet innocent baby...well, one look into those blue eyes and she knew leaving wasn't an option. Not yet.

Had Aunt Betty been trying to test Cara, to see if she could handle the situation, or was it because Aunt Betty had known there were ghosts?

Cara cradled the baby against her chest and opened the bag to get a good look inside. Diapers, formula, and a large box of condoms. A little late for that.

She unzipped the side compartments and found baby shampoo. "What do you say we get you all cleaned up."

Fifteen minutes later, she'd bathed the baby in the sink, put a normal diaper on him, and made a fresh bottle. Settling in the recliner, with a burp rag over her shoulder, she rocked him while he ate. His little fingers clutched around her pinky as he stared up at her with Caribbean blue eyes, confirming Cara's first assessment of Coop. He did make beautiful kids. The baby's eyes slid closed. He was probably as worn out as Cooper.

Cara set the bottle on the table and burped him, wiping at his mouth. She kept him in her arms and rocked him the rest of the way asleep.

Cooper jogged down the stairs, running a towel over his head. He'd showered and changed into a pair of track pants without a shirt. Her eyes tracked his movements as he neared. The tick-tock of her clock sped up as her libido danced a quick rumba. Women everywhere would rejoice if he donated sperm. She silently wondered what it might take for him to give her a few of his swimmers. Nope, not happening. No way was she unleashing another Cruz into this world.

She wasn't looking for a husband, just a donor. She compared men like she did ice cream toppings. Which one would give her the most delicious outcome? This guy screamed the perfect combination. Damn his last name, and damn the hormones the doc had her on that were still coursing through her system. They had her acting like a wanton hussy.

"How did you get Adam to sleep?" he asked, his voice only a whisper.

"I'm more than a pretty face with a weird job," she answered with a wink. What the hell was wrong with her that she was flirting with the devil's brother? Heat flooded her body. "I would have put him down, but I don't know which room has his crib."

"I don't have a crib," he answered.

"You should look into that," Cara said, easing out of the chair. "This little guy needs a room."

"Why?" Cooper asked. Folding a blanket, he then tossed it over the couch. "He doesn't live here."

Cara glanced down at the sleeping angelic face. "But he has your eyes."

"So does my sister. She's the reason I came to your office. She's the one missing."

"So Adam here is your nephew?" Cara asked, trying to keep the surprise from her voice.

"Mine too." A deep voice Cara knew all too well came from the direction of the door. Her ex, Eric, stood in the doorway, holding a pizza box in one hand and a six-pack of beer in the other. Cara's heart twisted as she tried to bite back an angry retort.

"And that's my cue." Cara gave a tight-lipped smile up at Cooper and gently placed the baby in his arms. "I'm sorry about your sister."

Cara grabbed her keys and headed for the door. Eric blocked her exit. "If you'd dressed like that when we were together, I never would have strayed."

"Apologize," Cooper demanded, coming to stand next to her.

"That's okay. He's right. Your brother is only attracted to sluts, and I look like one." Cara turned back to Eric and masked her inner turmoil with deceptive calm. "The thing is, I can go home and wash mine away. Can't say the same thing about your girlfriend."

"Wife." His brow rose. His eyes twinkled as if he was trying to turn a knife no longer in her chest.

"Even better." Cara grinned. The joke was on him. "You're saddled for life, or at least half of the equitable assets, whichever comes first. Good luck with that."

Cara slid past Eric, careful not to touch him. She'd moved past hate into acceptance a long time ago. She was still plenty pissed, but it was more at herself. Seeing him again just kind of confirmed it. Dating him had been a colossal mistake. Even colossal mistakes helped a spirit grow.

She opened her car door just as Cooper slowly approached. "I'm sorry for Eric."

"Don't be. You aren't your brother's keeper," she said, remembering her sister's words. Thank God Cara wasn't Quinn's.

"Please help me find her." His voice cracked in desperation, and his eyes pleaded. "I'll do anything; I'll pay you anything. You name it. Just touch her stuff and see if you can give me any clues where she might be."

"I don't want your money."

"If not for me, then for Adam. He deserves to have his momma."

She should have seen the kid card coming. Cara let out a lengthy sigh. "Fine, I'm going to need something personal of hers."

"I can do better. I can take you to her house tomorrow, and you can touch whatever you want."

Cara nodded. She could do this, not for Eric, but for Cooper and Adam. The quicker she was about helping, the quicker she could forget. Maybe she'd be rewarded with a halo to go with her horns. It could happen. "Pick me up at eight. I live at 544 Rhodes Avenue."

"Thanks." He went to touch her arm, and she eased away. His brows dipped, and he dropped his hand. "Sorry, I forgot."

Cara slid into her car, shut the door, and drove down the street. She glanced in the rearview mirror to find Cooper still watching. Unease swept through her body, as she thought about what answers she'd find.

"Please don't be dead," she whispered into the silence of her car.

Chapter 3

Cooper parked outside the yellow beach house. Sheer curtains drifted through the open windows and danced on the wind. He hadn't expected her to live on the beach. He'd thought her the more practical type, maybe a brick one-story in town near her office, or even something with a flashing sign that said Psychic On Duty. This place was normal, even quaint. He ran his hand over his face, half in anticipation and half in dread. He'd asked for this, even though he didn't believe her capable.

He got out of the car, headed toward the front door, and rapped his knuckles against the wood. He lowered his sunglasses to shield his eyes from the early warm sun as the beach breeze kissed his skin. He heard the movement inside and saw a tall figure approaching, making him do a double take at the house numbers again.

"Aye?" A tall man, wearing nothing more than a Scottish kilt, answered the door.

"Uh...does Cara Thornton live here?"

"Who's asking?" The man crossed his arms over his chest and tilted his head.

"Special Agent Cruz," Coop answered.

"Aye, you must be her ex. Quinn told me you might be sniffing around."

"Who is it?" Cara hollered from somewhere in the house.

"Cruz," he hollered back with his Scottish lilt. "Want me to challenge him to a dual and win back your honor?"

"What?" Cara's voice squeaked as she stepped around the corner dressed in a flowered sundress. Her hair was pulled back in a ponytail. Her sunglasses were perched precariously on her head. Her hazel eyes sparkled as she smiled. "No need. This is the *other* Cruz, but I appreciate the offer."

Cara slipped past the big guy and out onto the porch. "I'll be back in a while. Don't eat my brownies while I'm gone, or your ass will be sleeping on the beach tonight."

Cara shut the door and followed Coop to his SUV. "Who was that guy?"

Cara opened her own door. "That's Laird Ian McDougall." She smiled. "And he was serious about a dual, so don't ever agree."

They both got into the car and he started the engine. "He's a laird?"

"Yeah, he's got the big castle and an even bigger ego. Oh, and he's a horn dog too, but he brought me brownies, so I'm letting him stay."

As if that should have explained everything. Cooper didn't know why he expected a normal conversation with Cara. The laird was a big guy. One of his arms was almost twice the size of Cooper's, and that was saying a lot. "So you let anyone stay that brings you dessert?"

Cara chuckled. Her eyes sparkled with amusement, and a sweet tinge of pink covered her cheeks. "So where does your sister live?"

He didn't miss the change of conversation. He was trained in the art of understanding body language, and judging by Cara's, it was as if she was going to Sunday brunch with a long-time friend.

"About ten minutes away."

"Great. I have time to meditate." She lowered her sunglasses to cover her eyes and turned on the radio.

Cooper didn't touch the buttons. There was no need; the radio was on his station.

The music did little to ease the knots increasing in his stomach the closer they came to his sister's house. He knew what to expect. He'd scoured the home, as if it were a crime scene, looking for any clues that might take him to his sister, and he'd found nothing. Nothing in her phone records, credit cards, or anywhere else he'd looked. It was as if she'd walked away from her life, leaving her child behind. When he'd gotten the call from daycare, as the next person to contact in case of an emergency, he'd been told his sister hadn't shown up. That alone tipped him off that something was severely wrong. No way would she trust Cooper with his nephew's welfare. Not by choice.

He pulled up outside his sister's little house surrounded by the white picket fence. Cooper killed the ignition. "This is it."

Cara let out a deep exhale. "Cooper, I have to warn you. You might not like whatever answers I can give you."

"Any answers are better than none." That was the truth. If this had been a case he'd been working, it would have gone cold.

"Okay." She gave him a grim smile. "Let me explain some things before we go in."

Cooper held her gaze.

"Nothing I tell you will be admissible in a court of law."

"Okay."

"If I see a face, we have our own forensic sketch artist, and I'll call her in so we can do a composite for anyone you're looking for."

"Okay." His skeptical tone had her raising a brow.

"How I work is that I touch something your sister either used every day, or that meant something important to her, or even something she recently bought. I tap into her energy and get flashes of her life. It's kind of like flashes of pictures taken with a camera. If there are any important ones that look out of place, I'll tell you."

Cara opened the door, and he followed, thinking she was done. "And whatever you do, no matter what I tell you that I see...don't touch me. It breaks the connections and will make me see yours."

"Got it. No touching."

She slid out of the car and moved to stand beside him on the sidewalk. "And one more thing."

"There's more?"

"Yeah. When I see those pictures, I've been told I...." She shook her head. "Never mind."

"You what?" he asked, opening the gate and letting her pass.

"I may...I kind of...."

"Just spit it out," he said, sliding his key into his sister's lock.

"My body is sensitive to the vibrations, so much so that it looks like I'm on the brink of an orgasm, even though I'm not."

His mouth parted, and he paused with the doorknob in his hand. What did one say to that?

"It's easier to show you than explain."

He gave a single nod, walked into the small house, and stepped out of her way, not wanting to taint his sister's energy with his own. Goosebumps rose on his arms as he watched Cara walk around the living room. She kept her fingers clasped behind her back as she examined the home like someone visiting a museum. "Can I see her bedroom?"

"Yeah. It's this way."

He walked into Angela's room and stepped out of the way. Cara did the same thing she'd done in the living room. She walked around the space and even peered into the closet before stopping outside the bathroom. "Are you sure nothing's missing?"

"Positive," he answered, swallowing around the lump in his throat.

Cooper followed Cara into the bathroom. Her smile widened as she pointed to the toothbrush. "May I?"

"Knock yourself out."

"Toothbrushes hold a lot of energy. It's touched every day by the owner, but this one"—she pointed to the wrapper in the trash—"is new, so it should help me see only the recent events." Cara set her phone on the counter and hit Record.

"Good luck." The words sounded as though he'd swallowed chalk. Cooper braced himself, not sure exactly what to expect.

He watched as Cara picked up the toothbrush and closed her eyes. Her chest heaved as her breaths came out in pants. "Are you kidding me?"

He didn't know if he should answer, so he remained silent. She tossed her head back and moaned as her head moved from side to side. He didn't know how long they stood there. Every nerve in his body clenched tight as each minute ticked by. Cara clutched the sink counter with her empty hand and squatted in front of it, as if the toothbrush was draining her energy.

He moved closer. His hands hovered around her in case she lost her grip and he needed to catch her.

"She's alive," she breathed out as her erratic breathing slowed. Her eyes slid open, and she licked her lips. She picked up her phone and stopped the recording.

"What did you see? Do we need to call your sketch artist?"

"No." Cara's lips thinned, and her eyes narrowed as she moved toward him. He stepped out of the cramped space to avoid accidently touching her. "I know who she's with."

"Who?" Cooper demanded.

Cara held up her finger to stifle his questions before punching in numbers on her phone and holding it to her ear. "This is Cara. I don't have time to explain, but I need you to pull up Becca's credit cards and see if she's used them recently, then pull up her company cell phone and email me any recent calls she's placed." There was a pause. "Never mind why. Cancel all of my appointments this week. I'm going to be out of town."

"What the hell is going on?" Cooper asked as Cara slid the phone back into her pocket.

"Oh, she's clever. She must have known that I'd pick the toothbrush to work from. Of course, she would." Cara practically sneered as she tossed her hands up in the air.

"Cara, tell me what you saw."

Cara crossed her arms over her chest and tilted her head. "Does your sister believe in mediums and psychics?"

"Yeah, she's called your company before. So?"

"Soooo. When I picked up the toothbrush, I was given two pictures. One of your sister looking down at the toothbrush and the next looking at a woman holding up a sign. More specifically, that woman was my sister, Becca."

Cooper ran his hand through his hair. "Are you saying Angela is with Becca? Where? What did the sign say?"

"The sign read... No time to explain. Had premonition. Angela is in danger from her ex. We ran. Take Adam to Mom's and meet us where you lost your virginity. Her ex will be tracking us. Be careful." Cara cleared her throat and shook her head.

"Her ex is serving twenty in the state pen. That doesn't make sense." Coop pulled out his cell and sent a message to his partner to check in on his sister's ex to verify his latest activities.

Cara shrugged. "Be grateful we got that much out of my sister and she didn't try to leave the message in braille. Becca is the flower child. She's all about peace, love, and light. There's no way she'll be able to keep Angela safe, so we need to find them fast."

"That should be easy enough. Where did you lose your virginity?"

Cara cringed. "A resort on a little island off the East Coast."

"That sounds easy enough. What's the name and I'll book our flight."

"No need. We'll take the company jet. I don't like crowded, confined spaces. There are too many opportunities to touch people. Who's watching Adam?"

"He's at daycare."

"You need to drop me off to pack and pick him up, then meet me at my mother's. Her address is—"

"I know her address." Cooper watched the confusion cross her face.

"You do?"

"I did a background check on you."

Her eyes widened in astonishment. It was probably best that he left off the fact that he'd invaded her privacy when Eric and she started dating. He thanked his lucky stars that she didn't know that Cooper had been the one trying to talk Eric into breaking things off.

"I don't know if I should feel violated or impressed," she said, slipping past him and out of the room.

He pressed his lips together to keep from saying anything. The less she knew about his motives, the better.

Chapter 4

Cara's mother held Adam snuggled in her arms and kissed his forehead as Cooper and Cara's dad transferred the luggage from her car to his.

"Are you sure you know what you're doing? How are you going to find her?" her mother whispered.

"Maybe hire a skywriter or send up a flare? Ooh, or maybe I'll leave her a message in the sand." Cara had no clue how she was going to track down Becca. "Or maybe I'll look for people doing the downward dog."

"I'm serious." Her mother tsked.

"I have no clue how we're going to find them, but we've got to try. Becca's the reason his sister ran off in the first place."

"Becca's premonitions are extremely accurate. If she knows that the ex is going to chase them, then the chances are that it's true."

"I know. That's what worries me." Thank God her sister didn't have access to a gun. She'd probably shoot her toe.

"Look on the bright side, dear. Agent Cruz is a good-looking man, smart, and ambitious. He could be a good candidate for a sperm donor. Maybe while you're traveling, you can convince him to make a deposit, if you know what I mean." Cara's mother raised and lowered her brows in quick succession.

"I can find my own donor, and I can guarantee his last name won't be Cruz."

"If you say so, dear." Her mom kissed Adam's head. "Be careful and have a nice flight."

The flight had been nice. Good weather, decent company, and huge leather seats. The best part was no accidental touches. It would eventually happen. She was about as lucky as the dog chasing the rabbit around a track.

"Is the island everything you remembered?" Coop asked while grabbing their bags.

"Thankfully, no," she answered, slipping her sunglasses over her eyes. "I think for most of my stay I saw double. Alcohol is not my friend. It's lost some of its...magic."

"Sobriety will do that to you."

That was an understatement. Age had made her more cynical. Betrayals had hardened her against the prospect of conceiving the old-fashioned way and falling in love. She was hopeless, and was bound to end up just like Aunt Betty, only with Cara's luck, her hair dye wouldn't be a pretty pink. It'd turn the color of Pepto-Bismol.

"How about we get some rooms and hit the bar. You know what they say...the bartender knows and hears all." He walked beside her into the terminal.

The limo ride to the resort was quick. If she'd been back for any other reason, she might have enjoyed the scenery, seeing it for the first time without everything being doubled. Now it was impossible to enjoy the sweat gathering beneath her bra, or the way her sundress had to be held down against the ocean wind as they stepped out of the car among the hustle and bustle of tourists in front of the resort. She held her hand to her stomach to squelch the dancing butterflies. Each person walking by was a potential connection she didn't care to make.

Cooper grabbed both of their bags and stood next to her. "I was a blocker on the football team during high school. Do you want me to clear the path?"

She shook her head. "I can deflect most of the images if the touch is quick, but too many and it drains me."

"We'll make this quick." He headed into the lobby with her following on his heels. Several people skimmed her arm in passing as she tried desperately to focus on Cooper's back.

The lobby was filled with *old* people dressed in flower-printed shirts. It was as though they'd just stepped into the middle of a geriatric convention. She'd never seen so many of their age in one place. She wouldn't be finding her sperm donor here.

"Well, at least Angela and Becca will stick out like sore thumbs." Finding them should be a piece of cake. Cara sidestepped several people as they made their way up to the reservation desk, where a young woman stood behind the counter.

"We'd like a room," Cooper announced, pulling out his wallet.

"Do you have a reservation?" the blonde behind the counter asked.

"No," Cara answered.

"I'm sorry. We're all booked for the convention." She smiled sweetly while undressing Cooper with her eyes.

Cara exhaled a long breath. "Don't you have anything? He's FBI." Cara lifted her brows at Cooper. "Show her your badge. Chicks dig that." Cara leaned toward Coop without touching him.

"Not all," he grumbled under his breath.

"Oh, you must be here about the thefts." She clasped her fingers together. "We still don't have any rooms for you. Maybe you can try a hotel on the other side of the island."

A man stepped out from a room behind the counter. "Excuse me," he said as he approached. "Are you Cara Thatcher?"

Cara shared an uneasy look with Cooper. "Yes."

"They told me you'd come," he said, sliding the blonde woman out of the way. "Ms. Becca Thatcher showed me a picture of you. She reserved you a cabana and paid for it in advance."

"She did?" Cara smirked at the blonde, set her purse on the counter, and dug for her wallet.

"Lovely girl. She also left you a package," the manager-looking guy said.

He slid the package across the counter along with the paper for her to sign.

47

"Do you happen to know where I can find my sister?"

"Ummm. I'm afraid not. We've been a bit busy at the counter. You might try the pool area or the beach."

She picked up the brown-wrapped package and hugged it to her chest as Cooper took the keys. Oddly, no visions smacked her in the face. Not even whoever had manufactured the brown parcel.

"Ms. Thatcher mentioned you'd need privacy so she reserved the honeymoon cabana on the west side of the resort, and you have a private pool and a secluded part of the beach." He used a marker to draw a line from the lobby to the location on a map and handed it to Coop. "I hope you enjoy your stay."

Cooper remained quiet until they'd passed the guest pool area and were on the walkway toward the cabana. Trees from both sides of the walkway provided a shaded canopy from the sun. "It could be worse. We could be sleeping on the beach."

"I'm sure they picked that one since it's secluded and will give us privacy."

Cara raised her brow. She knew her sister. She'd picked it because she thought Cara might get lucky, or maybe it had the best Feng Shui. Becca's safety wouldn't even be a part of the equation. If it had been, Angela and she would have been staying in that room. Maybe they were.

The canopy of trees gave way to their cabana. It was like a little oasis away from the noise in the resort. The view was stunning. The décor was light and airy. The cabana would have been perfect, if it hadn't been for the reason they were there. A bed sat in the middle of the room. The position gave the occupants ease to gaze out of the floor-to-ceiling windows that opened. That bed was a baby-making bed, or maybe it had been made for giants. She could see herself having hot dirty sex on that bed. Too bad she was here with Cruz.

"Are you going to open the package?" Coop asked, pulling her from her thoughts of sweat-slicked bodies enjoying the beach breeze.

"Of course." She dropped her purse onto the bed. She ripped the package open and dumped the contents on the white comforter. An envelope, a red bikini, and a pair of flowery men's swim trunks tumbled out.

Anger stirred in her belly. If Becca thought for one minute that this was some kind of vacation, then she was more delusional than Cara thought.

"What the hell?" Coop asked, picking up the trunks while she ripped the envelope open. Instantly she was hit with her sister's vibration, and she started to pant and closed her eyes. Every fiber in her body tingled to life as the energies combined.

Becca stood in front of the mirror looking at herself as she held the paper and spoke. "Cara, I know you got this. We had to leave, but we'll double back on Sunday. Stay, so we know where to find you."

The scene cut off just as abruptly as it started. Cara's eyes flew open as she examined the empty sheet of paper and flipped it over to check the back.

"What did you see?" Cooper asked, hovering next to her as if he'd been about to touch her.

Before her legs could give out, Cara slid down onto the bed to catch her breath. The energy from fighting the crowded lobby, and now the letter, had drained her like she'd done to her morning coffee. "They had to leave and want us to stay until they return. They're going to double back."

"They're both nuts if they think I'm just going to sit around here until they decide to show back up."

"You're right, but I need to rest." Cara's shoulders drooped, and she exhaled a long, deep breath. The bed beneath her butt promised a comfortable snooze fest. "The energy from the lobby was too much."

"Did you get touched?"

She nodded and scooted up onto the bed, resting her cheek on one cool pillow and grabbing the other to snuggle with. They provided just the right support. Those two pillows would go missing when they left, even if she had to sneak one in her bag and the other beneath her shirt. It would give her practice maneuvering with a pregnant belly. "Let me just close my eyes for a little bit, and then we'll leave."

If he had a reply, she didn't hear it, as the sweet, silent darkness quickly worked its magic and pulled her into a restful sleep.

Chapter 5

Cooper left the cabana's floor-to-ceiling windows open so he could hear Cara when she woke. He was on his fifth lap in the pool under the moonlight. The cool water sluiced over his body as he worked at relieving the tension in his neck. How had he gotten to this point? He was stranded alone, with a crazy, psychic woman sleeping only a few feet away. His sister was going to get an earful when she finally showed back up. She should have come to him if she'd been scared, not some wishy-washy woman she'd probably found by dialing 1-800-NutJobPsychics on the phone.

Cooper emerged from beneath the water to hear Cara's cell phone blaring the death march for the fifth time in the last two hours. Weird was an understatement. The sound of the ringing stirred Cara awake, so Cooper continued swimming. He'd finished two more laps when he re-emerged into the shallow end to find her standing at the foot of the pool with the phone pressed against her ear.

"Did you know you talk in your sleep?"

She clicked the phone off and tossed her head back to look up at the moon. "Get used to it. It seems we're stuck here," she said with a sigh. "My mother left five messages. My dad had an emergency and needed the jet, so he called it back."

"There's more than one way off the island," Coop said, hoisting himself out of the pool. He grabbed a towel, ran it over his body and watched as her eyes followed the movement.

"You can go back. I'm going to stay and wait for Becca and Angela to return. I'll call you when they show." Cara spun in place and walked back into the cabana.

"That's ridiculous. We'll go back together and figure out another way to track them down. I've already got my FBI partner, Howard, trying to find a way to track their movements." Howard had started to gather both of their sisters' phone and credit card records. Maybe he'd found a lead.

Cara started digging through her suitcase and pulled out some clothes. "Becca's visions are never wrong." Cara clutched the clothes to her chest. "If she said she'll be back Sunday, then she will. I know you don't believe in her or me, and that's fine, but I believe in her, so I'm staying. I hope Howard and you enjoy your search, and I really do wish you luck."

She might as well have just asked him to believe in the tooth fairy. At least that would have been more believable. Cara headed toward the bathroom.

The room turned cool from the ice in her voice. Coop crossed his arms over his chest. "Why should I believe your sister?"

His question stopped her in her tracks. She slowly turned around and pegged him with her glare. She was getting pissed. Had no one ever questioned her judgment before? He'd seen that look a dozen times before. He knew what was coming next, and he braced for her words.

"Listen, I don't care what you believe. You came to me for help. Not the other way around. Our sisters are in danger, and I'm not stranding them to fend for themselves. If Becca said she'll be back, then she'll be back. I trust her visions, and I trust her. That's more than I can say about you."

"I'm not my brother, princess. So you can lose the bitchiness."

"Yeah, and I'm not your princess. I have a name, so use it."

"And come Sunday, when she doesn't show? We'll have wasted a week when we could have been searching for them."

"It's my week to waste. No one is keeping you here, Coop." Cara's lips pinched together as fire flickered in her eyes. He was one argument away from having to sleep in one of the patio chairs. He'd slept in worse.

Cara closed the bathroom door, and within minutes, he could hear the water running as she took a shower. It was going to be one hell of a long week.

Cara expected Coop to be long gone when she finished her shower, but she wasn't that lucky. She'd taken her time washing away the stress from the day, only to emerge fresh and clean to find Coop sitting outside under the moonlight, drinking a beer with the phone pressed to his ear. The smell of tomatoes drifted on the air, teasing her nose as she tossed her clothes back in her suitcase. Her stomach grumbled.

"Something smells good."

"Howard, I'll call you back. Keep searching."

Cara held her grin in check. It appeared Mr. FBI was having about as much luck as Coop and her. Becca was staying off the government radar? Maybe those conspiracy books she read had come in handy. Thank goodness, Cara hadn't given her *Silence of the Lambs*.

"I figured you'd be hungry, so I ordered us room service."

Ten minutes ago, she would have argued he was an insensitive jerk. Now he was offering her food. Had there been dessert, she might have apologized too. Cara slid into one of the chairs opposite him and lifted the cover from her plate to find a huge portion of lasagna with breadsticks.

"Italian is my favorite." And it showed on her thighs.

His lips twitched as he reached for the bottle of wine and poured her a glass. "Consider it my apology for being an ass."

"Trying to get me drunk, Coop?"

"Nope, just trying to help you relax."

She took a bite and moaned in satisfaction as a mixture of flavors burst in her mouth. With every savory bite, the tension in her shoulders dwindled a little more. As the herbs and garlic mellowed her, she tried to see Coop in a new light. A guy who ordered her favorite meal couldn't be all bad, right?

"You're very..." he started to say.

"Hard-headed?" she asked.

"Loyal," he corrected. "I wouldn't have guessed that."

Her brow rose, but she bit her tongue against starting another argument. Did he think she wouldn't be? "You did the same for your sister. It must have been hard to come ask for my help since you're a skeptic. Becca must have seen in a vision that you'd try."

He took a sip of his beer, his gaze shuttered, guarded, as if he wasn't sure how much to divulge. His food lay forgotten as he leaned back in his chair and tilted his head, as if studying her for the first time. Heat crept up into her cheeks, this time not from her temper but the way he watched her as she continued to eat. "I deal in facts. I believe in what I can see. What I can explain. Everything has a logical explanation; it has to in my line of work."

She'd heard his words a thousand times before. It was one of the main reasons Cara and her sisters didn't get involved in the cases unless requested by the authorities. They didn't understand, unless they wanted to, unless they needed too. His lack of acceptance bothered her more than it should, a feeling she wasn't ready to analyze just yet.

"Okay." Cara swallowed around her bite of bread. "Explain the gut feelings you get when trying to solve a case. Explain how it is that I knew they came to the island. Explain how Adam was floating in the air. Just because you can't see the things I can, it doesn't make them any less true."

Coop's brows dipped as he rubbed his chin. She was annoying him and picking at his resolve, but no matter what she said, or how she explained, he'd never truly understand and probably would remain a skeptic. It was his right. She wasn't here to change his mind. That would be like asking him to believe in mermaids. No one was perfect.

Cara finished eating in silence as Coop excused himself to take a shower. She took a quick walk down the beach and made a few calls to check on Ian to make sure he wasn't having an orgy. Then she called to check on Adam before she returned to the cabana. Coop was lounging on the bed in all his shirtless glory, the sheet pulled to his waist, teasing her imagination as to what might lie underneath. She couldn't deny that she was intrigued by him and his looks, more than she should be.

The light from the lamp played across his toned, tan abs, the dips and valleys disappearing under the linen in a rather enticing display. Cara swallowed hard and fought to lick her lips.

"There's only one bed."

"I know. I guess my sister didn't plan for everything." Cara walked into the room and grabbed a T-shirt from her bag. She turned her back and changed into the long shirt before discarding her shorts. She grabbed the extra pillows in the closet and stacked them down the middle to separate their bodies.

"No offense. It's not that I don't trust you." It was more like she didn't trust herself. When was the last time she'd slept next to such male perfection? With her luck, she'd molest him in her sleep, and her visions would go into overdrive, much like her hormones. None of his secrets would be safe.

His lips twisted up at the corners. "How do you do it?"

"That's a loaded question. You have to be a bit more specific," she answered, crawling into bed.

"How can you be intimate if touching someone wears you out?"

Cara shifted the covers over her abdomen, and she turned to face him, resting her cheek in her palm. "When I touch someone for the first time, I get flashes of their entire life: the good, the bad, and the ugly. It doesn't matter. Once the initial touch is over, then the next time that person and I touch, it's just like an update of the things that happened since the first touch, so it's less powerful and much quicker. It's how I knew your brother had cheated on me."

She swallowed around the lump in her throat and ignored the ping in her chest. It shouldn't still have the power to hurt her, yet every time she thought of it, the wounds broke open. She didn't know how much of it was because she'd thought herself in love with him, and how much was from the fact that she'd trusted the wrong man. Her gut instinct had malfunctioned, much like that one time she'd tried to light a grill. Her eyebrows still hadn't grown fully back.

"Must be hard for the other person to be so exposed and unable to keep anything secret or plan surprises."

Cara hadn't thought what it meant for the other person. "I guess."

"So I'm betting one-night stands are out of the question for you."

A smile split her lips. "You'd be right."

"Pity." He winked.

Pity? Was he flirting with her or mocking her? It was hard to tell. Rolling over, she stared up at the ceiling as his soft snores quickly filled the quiet, dark room. *Pity.* Why did that one word hold so much power? It had been awhile since she'd indulged in male's interest in her, so she was going to blame her sex-starved body for the reaction that one word evoked. She tingled in places that had lain dormant. She closed her eyes and couldn't help but wonder...what if.

Chapter 6

Cara's eyes flew open to the feel of a heavy arm draped over her stomach. The pillows that had separated them the night before were at the bottom of the bed. Her heart thumped wildly in her chest as she waited for the visions to hit, preparing herself for the flashes from Coop's life and the physical effects of having them. She clenched her eyes closed and braced herself.

Nothing. She blinked her eyes several times and turned her head. Coop was sound asleep. Had that been why she didn't see anything? The ladylike thing to do would have been to slip out of the bed and hope not to wake him, yet she couldn't move. The warmth of his arm pinned her in place, and she relished the feel, even savored it like a starved, deprived woman.

"Coop." Her voice came out in a whisper. Coop didn't budge.

She cleared her throat and spoke louder. "Coop."

Still nothing.

"Cruz," she said even louder. His sleepy gaze met hers.

"It's too early, Cara. Go back to sleep."

Nothing. He was awake, and there was no onslaught of visions, nothing from his life. "Cooper, you're touching me."

Coop's eyes shot open, and his body tensed before he yanked his arm away. "I'm so sorry, Cara. What did you see?"

"Nothing. I saw nothing." She stared at him in disbelief. No other human being had ever had the same effect.

Why had she not seen a thing? She couldn't fathom an answer in the uncharted territory. It left her both baffled and intrigued, fighting the urge to run her hands over every inch of his body. She'd never encountered a person who didn't trigger a vision.

"How is that possible? I thought you saw everyone."

"I do." Her voice squeaked.

She gestured to his chest. Her fingers itched to explore the hard planes, and for something other than a vision quest. *Remain focused. He doesn't need my fingers dipping below the waistband.* "May I?"

"I've worked a lot of bad cases and seen some gruesome things in my life. Are you sure you want to try again?"

She nodded. She had to know.

He took her hand and placed it firmly over his heart. His chest rose and fell beneath her palm. Nada. Zilch. She shook her head. What the hell had happened?

"Maybe you aren't doing it right." He rolled her until she was on top of his hard body. Any other woman would have giggled at the action, but not her. Even though she was perplexed by the absence of her visions, her body was very aware of his. The tingles were back, but she pushed them aside until she could figure out the mystery.

"Nothing."

He slipped his fingers into her hair with one hand and touched her cheek with the other as her body melded with his. She leaned into his touch as if searching for more contact. She'd never realized how much she missed the simple pleasure. "Now?"

"I don't understand. This doesn't make sense."

"Cara." The lines around his eyes softened. "Why are you immune to me?"

She shook her head as the tingles of desire melted away. Panic took hold and shook her like a Magic 8 Ball. Had the ability that she'd hated all her life just vanished overnight? Did that mean she was broken? It had been a part of her for so long, she wasn't sure she could survive without it. "I don't know."

Tears pooled in her eyes as she held his gaze. Fear seized her body, squeezing her heart. Without her ability, who was she?

"It's okay, Cara. Don't cry. Maybe it's just a fluke. Maybe the visions came when you and I were both asleep."

Adrenaline coursed through her veins, and she rolled off of him and jumped from the bed. Determination steeled her nerves as she grabbed a sundress from the bag and started to change, not bothering to even go into the bathroom. The need to find out what was going on won over her modesty. "You're right."

"Cara, where are you going?" Coop got out of the bed and pulled on shorts. He swiped a hand over his face. He'd thought she was crazy before, he was about to witness a full-out panic attack.

"I'm going to find someone else to touch," Cara said as she slipped on shoes and hurried to the door.

Coop laid his palm on her arm. Another sensation she hadn't felt in a long time. She glanced at his hand and was greeted with nothing but warmth. The sensation wrapped around her, and she caught herself leaning toward him, wanting more. She could kiss him. She shouldn't kiss him. Hell, even her mind was out of whack. "I don't want you going alone. Wait for me to put my shoes on."

She nodded, and within minutes, they were out the door. They didn't have to go far to find someone to touch. An old couple stepped out of the cabana closest to theirs and was headed toward the resort. She'd never been so happy they walked so slowly. Cara hurried up behind them and lightly touched the woman's arm. Fear and uncertainty plagued Cara as she prepared for a void where her visions once lay. "Excuse me? Can you point out the way to the restaurant?"

Cara had to concentrate on the sentence when her chest started to heave, and visions of the woman's life flashed before her eyes. The couple was so much younger. The husband was on one knee as he held out a small diamond ring and asked her to marry him. It switched instantly to her wedding day, standing in front of a full-length mirror in a lace wedding dress with the veil covering her face.

Coop rested his hand on Cara's arm, and the visions she'd just started to experience instantly began to fade.

Cara glanced at his hand and met his gaze. She was sure it showed in her eyes. He lifted his hand, and the visions started to return. Cara yanked her hand away as Coop pulled Cara back to his side. The warmth of his arm cocooned her. She'd never experienced anything like Coop's touch before. It made her feel...safe, protected and even somewhat vulnerable. Why him? Why now?

"The restaurant is just past the pool," the old woman announced. "You're welcome to follow us. That's where we're headed."

"Thanks, but I just realized I forgot my purse. We're just going to go get it."

"We'll save you a place at our table. I'm John, and this is my wife, Martha." The old guy smiled as he steered his wife away.

Coop waited until they were back inside the cabana before he asked. "Well? Anything?"

Cara nodded as she plopped down on the bed. "I saw up until her wedding, and then you touched me and they faded away. When you lifted your hand, they started back up. You somehow have the ability to make the visions stop."

"How about we finish getting ready and we go meet the old people and get some breakfast? We'll think more clearly with food in our systems. It will give you a chance to try out your ability on some other people."

She nodded, afraid to speak. What did it mean that Coop could dampen her psychic ability? Was it a good thing, or should she be running in the other direction?

John and Martha waved Coop and Cara over the moment they stepped in the door. Coop pulled out Cara's chair at the breakfast table and grabbed them both a menu as a waiter appeared to fill their water glasses. Cara and he were the youngest people in the restaurant. John wore a hearing aid in one of his ears. His white hair was the color of the beach sand, and Martha was a petite woman with hair curled so tight it looked like it hurt.

"We're so glad you made it." Martha smiled at Cara. "John didn't think you two would want to hang out with us geezers since you're on your honeymoon."

"Oh no..." Cara's cheeks blushed.

"She's still not used to being married. I had to practically carry her down the aisle, isn't that right, dear?" Coop scooted his chair closer and held her gaze. "Of course, we're married. Why else would we be on this beautiful island and staying in the honeymoon suite?"

Cara smiled and turned back to Martha. "Of course. Newlyweds. I'm still not used to being married." She lifted her bare hand. "I told him I wouldn't wear the three-karat ring he bought me, but you know men... They just won't listen."

Coop took Cara's hand and lowered it to the table. "Nothing but the best for you, baby."

Martha playfully smacked her husband's arm. "Did you hear that, John? He bought her a three-karat diamond wedding ring. You cheap bastard." Martha's sweet grin held a tinge of something he couldn't identify as she turned back to them. "The one he gave me was fake."

"Be lucky you got one at all, you old hag," John grumbled and sipped his coffee.

"Oh, he's just saying that," Martha said as she shoved her spoon into her grapefruit, stabbing it with zest, as though it was her husband's heart.

The waiter returned with his pad, took their order and brought them both some coffee cups.

"So...are you two just on vacation?" Cara asked, placing her palm on the woman's arm. Her breathing became rapid. Coop slipped his hand onto Cara's shoulder, and her rapid breath slowed. She glanced up at him. He could read the confusion on her face. It had happened again from a single touch. He sat up a little straighter and puffed out his chest. He could do something no other man could do. His cock hardened in response as he thought of the possibilities. If his touch didn't trigger visions, then it meant he could touch her everywhere. Maybe it wasn't as bad as he thought. He could give her that one-night stand she'd never experienced and still keep his secrets. A few nights of having Cara beneath him might make this week of waiting more interesting.

"We're here for the conference," Martha answered.

"Oh? What conference is that?" Cara asked and leaned back to make room for the server bringing their order of pancakes.

Coop took a sip of his coffee, enjoying the warmth sliding down his throat as Cara poured syrup over her stack of cakes. She drenched them until a pool settled at the bottom of the plate.

"The swingers conference of course."

Coop sputtered the coffee.

"Who do you guys build swings for, children?"

Martha chuckled, and her cheeks blushed. "No, dear. The swinging we do is much different."

Cara's brows dipped as she glanced at Coop. He couldn't hide the smile on his face. He leaned to whisper in her ear. Her hair smelled of sweet strawberries, momentarily making him forget what he'd been about to say. "She's talking about sex partners."

Cara's mouth parted, and her eyes grew wide before she quickly snapped her mouth shut. "Oh. Well. Of course. Those swingers."

Her cheeks flushed a pretty pink as she concentrated on her pancakes, occasionally glancing up and across the room to an old man eating alone.

"Uh..." She wiped her mouth with her napkin and grabbed her phone already pressing a button to record. "Will you excuse me for a minute?"

Coop grabbed her hand. "Cara, where are you going?"

She leaned down to whisper in his ear, acting as though she was going to kiss him. "I need to give a reading. That man's wife is with us in spirit, and he needs to hear a message from her. It's urgent. I'll only be a few minutes."

A few minutes turned into over an hour, and Martha and John had left in search of God knows what.

Coop paid the bill and walked over to where Cara was deep in conversation. The man she was speaking with was wiping tears from his eyes.

"She wants you to be happy," Cara whispered to the man and clicked the recorder off. "I'll send this to you as we discussed. You can replay her messages whenever you're feeling down."

"Cara, I don't mean to interrupt, but I'm just going to head back to the room."

The old man grabbed Coop's hand and squeezed. "You're a very lucky man. Cara has a beautiful gift. The validations she gave me about my wife, no one would have known. The messages she gave were needed. I'm truly blessed to have met her."

Cara's eyes were misty as she rose. "Don't give up, Harry. Promise?"

He nodded and dropped Coop's hand. "I promise."

Coop led Cara out of the restaurant and waited until they were back at the cabana before he spoke. "What was that about?"

"Harry's wife died three weeks ago, and he just found out he has cancer. She doesn't want him to give up, and I needed to tell him."

"You did your medium thing?" Coop asked as he shut the door.

"Yeah. He needed the message to help him heal. What was up with the newlywed cover?"

Coop shrugged as he moved to the windows looking out to the pool. "It's easier for people to believe that's why we're here than having to answer a million questions. So when you touched people, did you get images?"

"Every time you weren't touching me, I did."

Chapter 7

Cara sat on the edge of the pool, and the cool water swirled around her legs as she watched Coop swim laps. Her gaze swept over his muscular body propelling from one end to the other. Sweat beaded over her body, and an oppressive heat weighed her down, one not even the beach breeze could cool. Five more days of sun and relaxation. What the hell had her sister been thinking? Coop and she would be driving each other nuts within a day if she didn't jump him first. The muscles in his arms bunched with each stroke and kick of his legs. The bathing suit her sister had left hung low on his hips, teasing Cara with a hint of what lay beneath. Cara's breath hitched in her throat as she thought about the warm caresses of his fingers on her cheek earlier, and she realized she wanted more of that. More of Coop.

She'd buried herself in her work, and she'd forgotten how to just relax. She worried her bottom lip between her teeth. Sex with Coop would be different, freeing without the bombardment of visions. The thought intrigued her, not that he'd even suggested any interest.

Coop swam over to Cara and rested his hands on the ledge on both sides of her legs. "You're thinking too loud. Come in the water and cool off."

"How can you just swim like you're on vacation?"

Coop ran his hand over his wet head and stood to his full height between her legs. "What else do you expect me to do?"

"I don't know." That was the truth. She had no idea what to do. Her body was practically vibrating with nervous energy.

"We need a plan."

Cara released a breath she didn't realize she'd been holding. A plan, she could do a plan. She was great at organizing and making decisions, and maybe planning would keep her thoughts off Coop's body and what she'd like to do to it. "What do you have in mind?"

Coop rested his hands on her thighs. The move was innocent enough to any normal person. She glanced down at the connection, unfamiliar being touched without visions claiming her energy. She closed her eyes to hide her feelings. As much as she enjoyed his touch, why did it have to be him? He was a Cruz. Her body wanted him; she couldn't deny that, but her mind screamed that his brother had betrayed her in the worst way. Could she separate the two?

"What's wrong?" he asked.

She lifted her gaze to his. "Of all the people in the entire world, why are you the one that I'm immune to?" She couldn't hide the defeat in her voice.

"I don't think we'll ever know the answer to that question." His voice softened. "I'm sorry you're upset that I'm the one with the golden touch."

"Golden touch?" She smiled.

"Well, I call it like I see it," Coop said, lifting her from the ledge and dunking her in the water.

He cradled her in his arms as they emerged from the water. The refreshing liquid cooled her body and her mind while being pressed against Coop warmed her in other ways.

"Why'd you do that?" she asked, wiping the water from her face.

"You needed to cool off," he said as her body slid down his until her feet touched. "So about that plan..."

His words died off, and his face turned serious as he gazed over her head. "Can I help you?"

"Agent Cruz?" A male spoke behind her, and she slowly turned in Coop's arms.

"Yes?"

"Cara?" he asked, stepping forward. "I can't believe it's really you. It's good to see you."

Cara recognized him instantly. His brown hair was cut in a crew cut, and he was dressed in a hotel security guard uniform with a badge and a gun, but she'd never forget his face, no matter how many years had passed. Why would she? He'd been the one she gave her virginity to. "Phillip. It's been a long time."

Phillip's gaze lowered to her bikini top and lingered on her breasts before slowly returning to her face.

Coop's arms surrounded her as he leaned down and pressed his lips to her neck. "Do you know him, baby?"

Phillip held up his hand as he blushed. "I'm sorry, Cara. I don't mean to interrupt your honeymoon, but I need to speak to Agent Cruz. It's urgent."

Coop took Cara's hand and guided her to the steps and out of the water. He grabbed a beach towel and wrapped it around her body, covering it from Phillip's eyes before Coop grabbed his own.

It was comical that Coop was shielding her body from Phillip's eyes. He'd seen more of her goods than Coop had.

"What's so urgent?" Coop asked, running a towel over his head.

"One of our guests is missing."

More than one, but Cara bit her tongue instead of correcting him. They were on the island for the exact same reason. Were they related?

"Did you call local law enforcement?" Coop asked.

"Yeah. They're already looking for him, but they're spread thin with the rash of burglaries on the island."

"Oh, that's right. Didn't the desk clerk mention the thefts when we checked in?" Cara asked, stepping up next to Coop. "Maybe we should...help, in case...you know."

Coop glanced down at her with his brows pinched.

"Phillip, could you excuse us for a minute?" Cara asked.

"Sure." He glanced between Coop and Cara as she pulled Coop into the cabana and shut the door. His handsome face was reserved, making her falter in the silence that engulfed them.

"What gives?"

"We have to help find the guest. It's the right thing to do."

"I'm not on the clock. I came here for one purpose, Cara, to find my sister."

"The disappearance could be related. We won't know unless we help."

Coop crossed his arms over his chest. "How do you know Phillip?"

"Seriously?" Cara's lips twitched in amusement that he hadn't already figured it out. He must severely suck at his job, unless he was playing stupid for a reason. "I lost my virginity to a local, and he's the only local I know."

Coop moved toward her until he had her back pressed against the door. "Are you going to try and rekindle that flame?"

"Why would that matter?" Cara gasped as he leaned in. She curled her fingers to keep from holding him closer. Her body went up in flames every time he was near, whether she liked it or not.

"I can't have my pretend wife hot for another man." His breath fanned hot against her ear. "Relax, Cara. I'm teasing. I know whose touch you crave."

His words, no matter how true, reminded her that confidence rolled off him in waves. "I don't know." She shrugged as a smile played on her lips. "It might be nice to catch up on old times." She slid beneath his arm and peered out the window. "I can always tell him we split up after we left the island and come back."

Coop moved behind her and rested his hands on her hips, pressing the length of his hard body against her.

She wiggled her ass against him and laughed. "You're playing with fire the way you keep striking that match. Not a good idea unless you're prepared to whip out a hose."

"I can give you something he'll never be able to do."

"What's that?" she asked as her ovaries danced the cha-cha. The war had been waged. Her body was screaming *give it to me hard,* but her mind was perched atop a ten-foot wall and hanging on for dear life. Falling to the ground would hurt, but what a pleasurable way to go.

"A week of hot sex without the visions."

Heat pooled between her thighs. His touch sent a shiver up her spine as the blood in her veins heated to a boil.

His lips caressed her ear as he spoke. "Think about it. One week of the best sex of your life, and then, when it's over and we've got our sisters, you go back to being you, and I'll go back to being me. No strings attached."

Cara turned in his arms and rested her palms against his warm chest. The muscles flexed under her fingertips, making her want to explore. "You think I'm easy? You think that promises of hot, meaningless sex with you can persuade me?"

"No, Cara. I don't think you're easy. I think you want me. I can see it in your eyes. Feel it in the way your body leans into mine. I don't think you want me. I know you do." Coop wrapped his arms around her body, pulling her tight against him, and pressed his hard length against her body. "I think I want you too."

I think I want you too. Dude needed to work on his pick-up lines. That was worse than something an eighteen-year-old nerd with pimples would say. She wasn't a badge bunny. "Despite the great offer you are making, I think I'll pass. That was a solid six though." She rounded up. "Using your body to entice me was a nice touch." She winked.

"A six, really?" His lips twitched, and he tilted his head, amusement shining in his eyes.

"Really." Cara smiled up at him and patted his chest. "When seducing a girl, it's important to make her believe you're hot for her too." She stepped around him and opened the door. "Phillip, I'll help you find the guy. Just let me get cleaned up and dressed."

"Perfect." Phillip's eyes twinkled. "Is Agent Cruz going to help?"

Coop stepped out of the cabana. "Of course. You know, a happy wife is a happy life."

"Of course." Phillip's glanced between them both before settling on Cara again. "I'll meet you in the lobby in fifteen minutes?"

Coop wrapped his arms around her waist and pressed a hot, tender path of kisses down her neck. "Better make it thirty."

"Right." Phillip pointed with his thumb over his shoulder. "I'm going to go and check in with the others to see if they've found anything."

Cara gave Phillip a small smile as she watched him leave.

She spun in Coop's arms and stepped away from his touch. "Why did you do that?"

Coop shrugged. "We're honeymooners. He's got to know we can't keep our hands off of each other. It's to be expected, and just so you know...I've wanted you since I saw you in the bikini." He took her hand and placed it on his crotch. "I've got more than your six, right here." He winked back.

She rolled her eyes, stormed back into the cabana, and grabbed clothes from the suitcase. No matter how attracted she was to this Cruz, he had another thing coming if he thought she'd be an easy conquest.

She headed for the bathroom to change. No reason to give him any other chances to try and convince her that he was right. She already knew he was. It didn't mean that she had to like it. A one-night stand with him was tempting. The moisture between her thighs wasn't from the heat or the pool. It was from his touch.

Cara came out of the bathroom to find Coop waiting on the bed, fully dressed. "I'll make you a bet."

"Oh, I can't wait to hear this one."

"If I find the guest before you, you're mine for the rest of the week. One week of mindless, no-strings, sizzling sex."

"And what do I get if I win?"

"What do you want?"

Sperm immediately popped into her mind, not that she'd ever tell him. She wasn't the kind of girl to trick any man into helping her get pregnant. What did she want? "The truth."

Coop's eyes clouded. His hesitation spoke volumes. "About what?"

"Well. I can't read you like other people. So any time I ask you a question, regardless of how hard it may be to answer, I want the truth, no holds barred. That's my terms."

"Deal. If I find the guest, I have you and keep my secrets. You win, you have me and the truth to any and all of your questions. Do we have a bet?"

"Uh, I didn't say I wanted you," she clarified. "You added that."

His grin grew as he rose from the bed and closed the distance between them. "Deal or no deal, wife? I get to have you, my way, *or* you get me and the truth. I'm going to win you over, Cara. It's inevitable. It's just a matter of whether you get my honesty in the process."

Cara licked her lips as she stared up into his mysterious blue eyes. She could think of worse ways to spend a week than having Coop between her thighs. Getting him to tell her the truth was intriguing. Could she handle his honesty?

"Deal." She choked out her response.

Coop pulled her flush against his body and pressed his lips to hers. He teased her lips until she opened and moaned as he invaded her mouth. Their tongues danced and tangled, the sexy officer obviously bent on seduction. Lust consumed her body from the single kiss, making her hormones rage and her knees weak.

"That was just a preview." He released her, grabbed her phone, handed it to her, and then slipped his fingers through hers. "Let's go find our missing person."

KATE ALLENTON

Chapter 8

Phillip showed them into the missing guest's hotel room.

"His name is Marco Griffin," Phillip announced as Cara paced the room with her hands clasped behind her back.

"Was he here with anyone?" Coop asked, drawing Phillip's attention away from Cara as she seemed to be looking for something to touch.

"He's a speaker at the convention."

Cara's gaze met Coop's.

"What was he speaking about?"

Phillip cleared his throat before answering. "Pleasing your partners and fantasy sex rooms."

Coop covered the smile with his hand. "And how old is this guy we're looking for?"

"Thirty-five."

"That's young considering the rest of the guests," Cara announced, stopping in front of the computer on the bed.

Phillip's cheeks flushed. "He uh...he's apparently an authority on the subject."

"Maybe you should sign up for his lecture, honey." She beamed a bright smile at Coop.

Coop smirked. "Are you sure he's missing and hasn't just hooked up with one of the other guests?" Coop asked as he rubbed the stubble on his chin. Chances were the guy was shacked up in one of the rooms or got so involved in a private demonstration that he'd lost track of time.

"No one has seen him since the meet and greet, and he missed his slotted time to talk at the convention," Phillip answered.

"Can I see the surveillance?"

"Sure." Phillip walked to the door. "Are you coming, Cara?"

"I'll meet you in the lobby. I'm going to see if I can find anything on his computer."

Cara sat on the bed and smiled at Coop. She was about to use her ability and gain the upper hand. Phillip walked out of the room, and Coop paused to wink at Cara. "Good luck, wife. Don't stay too long looking at his porn."

"I don't need luck, and it's not me that needs porn, honey. It's you. You could stand to learn a thing or two." She winked back, picked up the laptop, and sat it in her lap. Her eyes shut, and her chest heaved. The look was erotic, and he'd planned to be the one to make that look happen again. He shut the door behind him to find Phillip waiting by the elevator.

Phillip led him into the security room to follow the cameras in search of Marco. He spotted him in the lobby and followed him to the elevators.

"Where's the rest?" Coop asked. "I assume you've got video on all the floors."

"I'm afraid that's all we got. Our security system went down, and we've had techs trying to bring it back up and restore the system."

Cara closed her eyes as the visions took hold and she was greeted by a good-looking man working on his presentation. Pictures of what she believed were sex playrooms and such crossed the screen as he looked at them, followed by porn with worse pick-up lines than Coop's. Then Marco...fondling himself.

She tossed the laptop and opened her eyes. Her cheeks heated from the vision. She got up and walked into the bathroom. The man's toothbrush was on the counter. She touched it and closed her eyes. Marco was looking in the mirror as he brushed his teeth. There was a knock on the door, and he continued to brush as he opened the door.

"You've got to be kidding," Cara swore as she recognized Marco's guest. She'd recognize that blue hair anywhere. "Aunt Betty."

Aunt Betty winked as if it were meant for Cara before the vision broke.

Cara left the bathroom, took the stairwell down into the lobby and went right up to the desk where the man who'd checked her in yesterday was standing. "Excuse me."

"Ah, yes, Mrs. Thornton, or is it Cruz? Your sister said you'd answer to both."

Nice. She swallowed around her retort. "Thornton is fine." She smiled sweetly. "Can you tell me what room my aunt is staying in? Betty Thornton."

"She said you would ask." The man smiled as he stroked the keyboard. "She gave me permission to give it to you. She's in Room 259."

"Perfect, thank you." Cara turned to leave and then spun around. "Could you tell Phillip and Agent Cruz in the security room to meet me up at that room. Tell them I think I found what they were looking for."

"Sure."

Cara jogged up the stairwell to the second floor and followed the room numbers to 259. She banged on the door. "Aunt Betty."

No answer. She banged again. "Aunt Betty, answer the damn door."

The door swung open just as Coop and Phillip approached. Aunt Betty was standing in a pink-feathered robe. "Cara. What a nice surprise."

"Where is he?" Cara demanded and pushed her way into the room to find Marco tied to the bed with a blindfold over his eyes. Thankfully, the sheet covered his groin.

"Betty...did you invite another woman? Remove my blindfold and let me see the tasty morsel."

"My wife is off-limits," Coop announced, removing the guy's blindfold.

Marco glanced between them both. "The more, the merrier. You can play too."

Cara ignored them both and turned to face Aunt Betty. "What are you doing here?"

"I'm here for the convention." She smiled sweetly. "Why are you here?" She rested her palms on Cara's arm. "And with Agent Cruz?"

Cara pressed her lips together as humiliation blossomed in her chest. She couldn't answer Aunt Betty truthfully, not with Phillip in the room. She also couldn't use the cover of a honeymoon without her questioning the answer. Deflection was needed. "Marco missed his speaking engagement."

"No, I didn't." Marco sat on the bed, rubbing his wrists that had been tied. "That's not until tomorrow."

"Uh, no, sir. That was last night. The seminar committee rescheduled you for tonight and replaced your time slot last night that you missed. They were worried about you, and we've been searching for you ever since."

Marco rose, pulling the sheet with him from the bed. He wrapped it around his body and walked over to Aunt Betty and cupped her cheek. "You were amazing, my bella. We'll pick up again tonight after the seminar?"

"Afraid not." Betty kissed him smack on the lips. "I'm going to spend some time with my niece and then head back to Florida. But thank you for the invite."

Betty was giving the guy the boot and Marco looked as though she'd just told him his performance was subpar. Just wow. Cara didn't know if she should be embarrassed or impressed.

Marco grabbed his clothes and disappeared into the bathroom.

"I'm going to inform the others that he's been found," Phillip announced.

"Good luck with that." Coop patted his back.

"Betty, you've got some explaining to do." Coop crossed his arms over his chest and tilted his head.

"What? I was here for the conference and knew you two were here, so I was going to kill two birds with one stone: check in on you and find some new toys."

"How did you know we were here?" Cara asked.

"Well, your mother, of course."

She walked over to the door and held it open. "Dinner, drinks, and dancing tonight. Meet me inside the restaurant at seven so we can catch up."

"Are you kicking us out?" Cara's mouth parted.

"Yes, dear." Betty grinned. "Unless you'd like to stay and watch me stroke Marco's...ego."

Cara held up her hands. "Nope. No stroking for us. You can explain later. Come on, Coop."

Betty stopped Coop from leaving and thrust a bag into his hands. She winked.

"You should have listened to me sooner. You're going to need these."

Coop opened the bag and glanced inside as a smile split his lips. "Did you have a vision?"

"Didn't need to." Aunt Betty smiled. "I can see it in your eyes. I have to warn you though. When you think you know everything...you don't, and when it comes to Cara, you only get one shot. Don't forget that."

"Okay, he's heard enough," Cara said, grabbing Coop's arm and dragging him from the room.

Cara pulled the hotel door closed behind them with a click and walked silently down the hall. She waited until they were past the pool to ask the question that was pressing on her mind. Aunt Betty being on the island was curious enough, and she may never get the answer to that question, but the bag? That one she could easily enough figure out.

"What's in the bag?"

Coop tossed his arm around Cara and handed it to her. "Take a look."

Cara peered inside, and her cheeks heated as she pulled out a box of extra-large ribbed condoms. "Nice. She must think you're hiding a bazooka in your shorts."

Coop squeezed her shoulder and leaned down to whisper in her ear. "She knows it's inevitable."

"I wouldn't be getting too cocky there, stud. She probably used a needle to poke holes in them."

Coop pulled open the cabana door. His brows dipped. "Why would she do that? Is she hoping I knock you up?"

Yes. Not that Cara was about to explain. That was probably exactly what Aunt Betty had in mind. Damn woman. She didn't want to have to explain why she'd made the comment, not that he'd understand. Coop wasn't father material. Watching him with his nephew proved that. "When dealing with Aunt Betty, there's no reason to her actions. It's best to err on the side of caution."

"Duly noted." Coop tossed the box and the bag into the trash, walked across the room, and pulled out another box of condoms from the bedside table. "Perk of the honeymoon suite. They seemed to have it stocked."

"I won the bet," she announced.

"I know. I promised to be truthful." He held her gaze as he answered. The color of his eyes deepened. "What do you want to know?"

Chapter 9

Cara moistened her lips as she pressed her back to the door, the coolness of the surface seeping through her shirt. An infinite number of questions swarmed her mind, but only one passed her lips. "Do you think I'm pretty?"

"No, Cara." Coop visibly swallowed. "I think you're beautiful."

"Are you saying that so I'll sleep with you?"

His lips twitched. "No. I'm being honest, just like I promised."

"Do you think my ability makes me a freak?"

Coop ran his hand through his hair as unease covered his face. He did. But would he be honest about it? She waited, unmoving. His answer determined how the next few days played out. Either they'd be having sex hanging from the chandelier, or he'd be packing a pair of blue balls. She wouldn't make it easy on him either.

Coop crossed the room and rested his palm on her cheek. "I *think* that you're complicated. I *think* that it's a shame you avoid physical contact. I *think* that you genuinely try to help people. I *think* you've proved enough for me to give you the benefit of the doubt. So the answer is no, Cara. I don't think you're a freak, just beautifully complicated."

Beautifully complicated like a painting with brilliant colors or paint by numbers? It didn't really matter which. That description really did fit.

A sensuous light passed between them. A delicate thread started to form between them. There was a tingle in her stomach and a jolt to her pulse. The startling fire blazing in his eyes heated her body as his gaze raked over her face and landed on her lips.

He wanted her, and she held the key to a night of naked Twister. All it would take is saying yes, and he'd ravish every inch of her body. She leaned into his touch and closed her eyes. No visions. Nothing. Why him? Why was he so special?

He was slowly breaking down her resolve, and he was right. No way could she handle six more days on the island with the looks he was giving her. No way could she handle the sexual frustration. Damn him. No strings attached. Not seeing his secrets leveled the playing field more than she liked. Silently she realized that she relied on her ability of knowing, even more than she'd thought. What would her life have been without her special gift? Would she be married to the wrong man? How many more mistakes would she have made?

"You're thinking too much." Coop's voice was a whisper against her ear.

His body was there for the taking. Just one word and they'd both find release. "Since you were honest with me, let me be honest with you."

Coop kissed her neck. "Okay."

His touch made it difficult to think as he pulled her body flush against his.

"I don't date cops."

"We aren't dating." He continued a path down her neck as he threaded his fingers through her hair.

"I don't know how to do one-night stands."

"You could, with me. You've never had one without the intimacy of having the visions." Coop's hand slid down her backside, and he pressed their bodies together. "I can wait, for now, but mark my words. I'm going to get you out of your head if it's the last thing I do. I think you need it more than you realize."

"What are you going to do?" she asked as he stepped back.

"I promised you honesty, but don't make me answer that." He released her. Her neck felt cold from the absence of his lips. Her pulse skittered at what he might plan. Coop was oblivious to it all.

He crossed the room and pulled out dress pants, a shirt, and a bag of toiletries. "It's a surprise that I think you'll enjoy."

Cara took a deep breath and gave him a worried smile before watching him walk into the bathroom. What the hell was he doing to her?

She needed to catch her breath. She needed the sexual tension in her body to dissipate, and fast, or they'd never make it to dinner with her aunt. She'd be too busy seducing him. Cara grabbed her phone and knocked on the bathroom door. "I'm going to step outside and make some calls."

"Don't stray too far. You need to get ready for dinner."

"I'll be quick." She walked out the door and sat in one of the lounge chairs. The evening breeze kissed her skin as she took a moment to regain her composure before she dialed Becca. The phone went to voice mail. "You need to call me back as soon as you get this."

She ended that call and called Harper. That sister answered on the first ring.

"What's up, Cara? Did you find her?" Harper asked.

"Nope. She left me a message though that said she'd be back on Sunday. Have you heard anything?"

Harper was silent.

The silence hung like a noose around Cara's neck. At any given moment someone would tighten it. "What aren't you telling me?"

Harper let out a lengthy sigh. "Um...I didn't hear from her, but we did as you asked and we tracked her credit card and phone calls."

"And?"

"She called Mom."

"What?" Cara sat up and squeezed the phone in her grip. "When? Have you talked to Mom?"

"I just hung up with her."

"Well?"

"Becca and Angela are safe. Trust me on that."

A relief like nothing else swept through Cara's entire body. The tension in her shoulders drained instantly. "Great. We'll be on the next boat out. Where are they?"

"Um...there's more to the reason Becca called."

"Well?"

"She had another vision. Your eggs were accidently destroyed. She wanted Mom to break the news to you if the clinic hasn't called you yet."

Destroyed eggs she could deal with. Her sister in danger was a whole different level.

"Not a problem. I'll freeze more. Where are Becca and Angela?"

"On their way to Mom's."

"Thank God. Thanks for letting us know. We'll head back tomorrow." Clouds formed over head as the sky darkened. "Hey, do me a favor and check in on Ian. He's staying at my house."

"No problem. Oh, and hey, Cara."

"Yeah."

"You're on a beautiful island with a good-looking man. Try and enjoy your last night there. Everyone is safe."

"I'll try."

Cara clicked the phone off and said a prayer as she glanced up at the night sky.

Cooper had the towel wrapped around his waist. His clothes were laying on the bed and he planned to get dressed in the room since he'd forgotten his boxers before getting in the shower. Cara walked into the room. Her eyes ran over his naked body, and she licked her lips. Did she even realize she had? A grin spread across her face, and her smile brightened.

"Becca called my mom, and she and your sister are heading back home. She must have seen they'd be safe."

"I wonder what changed." Coop muttered beneath his breath.

"Who know, I'm just glad it did." Cara wrapped her arms around his waist and rested her head on his chest. He ran his hand down her back, the heat from her body scorching his fingertips. His hopes of breaking Cara down to finally say yes were dwindling by the second.

"We have a reason to celebrate." Coop cupped her cheek and pressed a hot kiss to her tender lips. That had been the entire reason they'd come to the island, although he'd enjoyed planning in the shower what he'd had in store for Cara. He hadn't been kidding when he said he'd get her out of her head, and he had one night to prove it.

Cooper leaned into her, letting her feel his cock as he savored her lips. She needed him to make good on his plans. She just didn't realize it yet, but she would. With the threat against his sister momentarily forgotten, he let himself get lost in Cara's taste.

He teased her tongue as heat spread through his body. There would be no denying his desire, and by the time he was done with her, she'd be begging him to take her. He slowly broke the kiss and held her hazy gaze. "Go get your shower."

She nodded as if unable to speak. He'd have her screaming before they rested their eyes. She grabbed a dress and walked into the bathroom. Cooper waited until he heard the shower before he picked up the phone and called the concierge with his request, and then he called the swingers committee to see if they could help accommodate with a blindfold. They'd been all too happy to oblige.

The stuff he wanted arrived while she was still in the bathroom getting ready. He pocketed one of the items to use at dinner before canceling their plans with Betty. He made new dinner arrangements. He'd planned a night she wouldn't forget. It was because of her that his sister was safe, and he knew exactly how to repay her. After all, he had the golden touch, might as well put it to good use.

Cooper stood in front of the window staring out at the ocean beyond their pool. Waves crashed against the shore as the moon hid behind the clouds. He'd been lost in thought when Cara opened the door, stepping out of the bathroom in a little black dress and three-inch heels. Her hair was in waves going down her back, and his fingers itched to run through the silky strands. Her legs were bare and tan. She made him hungry, and not for the food he had waiting. She smiled, making his cock jerk.

"How do I look?" she asked. "Remember you're still being honest."

"Honestly?"

She nodded, and he could see the hesitation in her eyes.

"As great as that dress is, it would look better pooled around your feet. Should I show you?"

A blush crept into her cheeks. *That's it, Cara. I'll see your entire body do that before the night is over.*

She cleared her throat. "I'm starved."

He grinned and lifted his brow. "I am too, but that will have to wait until after our plans."

Her cheeks darkened from the light pink to a rosy shade.

Coop moved to stand in front of her and leaned in to whisper in her ear. "I promised you a night you'll never forget."

Her breath hitched, and her chest heaved against the fabric of her dress. "If anything I do frightens you, or you want me to stop, all you have to do is say the word; otherwise, I won't. Tonight is about getting out of your head and just feeling the pleasure. Pick a safe word."

"Excuse me?"

"A word that you wouldn't normally say, that when I hear it, I'll immediately stop whatever it is I'm doing."

"I.." She shook her head.

"What vegetable do you hate most?"

"All of them."

His lips twisted into a smile.

"Pick one."

"Squash."

"If I hear squash, I'll stop. Otherwise, tonight is about experiencing pleasure." He slipped her earlobe into his mouth and gave it a gentle tug. "Say you understand, Cara."

She nodded.

"I need to hear it. Tell me you understand."

"I understand. Cooper, this is a bad idea. I'm not sure what you're in to, but I've never...had need of a safe word. And why would I only get one? Why couldn't any vegetable stop whatever it is you have planned?"

Coop moved behind her and rested his hands on her hips. He slowly slid them down her side, inching her dress up against her body. "Fine, you can use any vegetable. Are you going to use one now?"

"No." Her body trembled as he lifted the dress higher.

"Good. No panties." His words were hot in her ear as he slid his fingers beneath the elastic and lowered them down her legs, letting the dress fall back into place. "You won't need them."

Her breath caught as he slowly stood and pulled her back against his chest, letting her feel exactly what he had in store for her.

"Promise me one thing." She lowered her gaze. "Promise me, no sex without a condom."

"You have my word," he said, stuffing her panties into his empty pant pocket and then patting the other one to make sure the blindfold was still in place before taking her hand. He led her out into the night and fresh air. The urge to bend her over and take her in the room had him raging hard. "I promised honesty, and honey, you're about to experience it first-hand."

"Oh God."

He laced his fingers with hers as they strolled toward the hotel. "Relax, Cara."

"How am I supposed to do that?" she asked and lifted her brow.

He pulled her to a stop and against his chest. "Do I need to take the edge off?"

Her bright eyes widened, and she licked her lips. That was the only answer he needed. Instead of heading inside the hotel, he pulled her into one of the pool tents and closed the curtain. He held her head and kissed her hot mouth as he slipped his hand under the hem of her dress.

Cooper ran his hands over her bare pussy. Her body trembled from his touch, making his cock jumped in anticipation. He slid his fingers between her slick folds. He swallowed her moan as he slipped his fingers inside of her. She was wet and needy, and it took every bit of his resolve not to take her where she stood.

He broke the kiss but held her gaze. "You have to be quiet."

Her breath caught again as her cheeks reddened. "Then you might want to remove your hand."

He grinned and inserted another finger with the first, making her bite her lip as her eyes slid closed.

She clenched his fingers as if in search for more, and it pained him not to give her exactly that. His cock pressed hard against his zipper as he continued the slick slide in and out of her channel, soaking his finger.

He rubbed her clit with his thumb until he could feel her spasms start. He took her lips again as she clenched his shoulders, digging her nails into his skin. He pressed on the bud and devoured her moan as her orgasm hit. He continued stroking her until she became limp in his arms, only stopping when her hooded eyes slid open.

"Now I know how to keep you quiet." As if the words turned her on, her fingers clenched him again.

She nodded. "And I might need to practice my screams just to get you to do it again."

"Better start warming up those vocal cords." He eased his fingers free and slipped them into his mouth, sucking her juices. He moaned. "I know what I'm having for dessert."

Cooper grabbed one of the towels from the stack and cleaned the evidence from her skin. "How did that feel without any visions?"

"Incredible." Her words were laced with desire. Exactly what he wanted, and they'd just begun.

Chapter 10

Cara had turned into a wanton hussy. She craved his touch and the way he made her feel. They stepped out of the pool cabana and Cooper tossed the towel in the dirty towel bin as he took her hand again. She'd been nervous before when he'd taken her panties. She'd been wanton when he had touched her. She was out of her mind for agreeing to this game.

Squash had been on the tip of her tongue when he'd kissed her before touching her. Heat pooled in her belly as she fought to slow her breathing as Cooper led her into the hotel, making a point to maneuver her so that no one accidently touched her. He leaned to whisper in her ear as they waited by the concierge desk.

"I'll be the only one stealing your energy tonight." He winked before the man approached. "Ah, Mr. and Mrs. Cruz, right this way. We've been expecting you."

"I thought we were meeting Aunt Betty." Cara glanced over her shoulder.

"I canceled." He slipped his fingers through hers and led her into the dining room and to a set of double doors. "Is everything ready?"

The concierge glanced between them and nodded.

"Good. I'll take it from here," Cooper said and moved in front of Cara. "Close your eyes, Cara, and keep them closed."

She closed them and then peeked through her lashes.

He leaned in to whisper, "Which vegetable is it going to be?"

Cara pressed her thighs tightly together to ease her throbbing clit. "You're being bossy."

"And I bet you like it." He smirked.

Cara clenched her eyes closed. She heard the click of the door before Cooper eased her into the room. The door clicked closed behind them. She heard the unmistakable sound of a lock being clicked into place. "Keep them closed."

She fought the urge to open them when she felt something silky being tied around her head. He rested his palms on her arms, making her jump.

"Relax," he whispered into her ear. "It's just a blindfold, and we're alone in a private dining area. Do you trust me?"

"Hell if I know why." She nodded and inhaled a deep breath before releasing it. "I trust you, but let me remind you that you're supposed to be honest with me. Any question I ask."

"I remember. Do you have any questions?"

"Did you lock the door?"

"Yes," he said, leading her through the room. She held her hands in front of her, afraid she'd bump into something.

"What are you going to do?"

"Feed you first, and then I'm going to eat."

He released her for just a second when she felt something lightly touch her legs. "It's a chair. I'm going to help you sit."

Cara eased down until she felt the chair with her fingers before sitting.

"What are you going to feed me?"

"There's no fun in that," he said as his voice got farther away. The unmistakable smell of strawberries drifted to her nose. "Open."

She did as he asked, and her tongue came into contact with something creamy. "Bite."

She did and was rewarded with the burst of strawberry and something cool and familiar like whipped cream. "This is good."

He continued with his game of letting her guess a variety of foods, and she even got accustomed to his touch and the idea of him feeding her. As foreign as the concept was, she enjoyed it all. He'd fed her fruit, bread and even some more of the lasagna before rewarding her with chocolate cake. She'd guessed them all correctly, and the tension from her shoulders eased.

"Why the smile?"

"I'm enjoying this."

"Are you full yet?"

She licked her lips. "I couldn't eat another bite."

"I could." His fingers touched her knees and he eased them open. "Scoot to the edge of the chair, Cara."

Her fingers tightened around the seat. "What are you going to do?"

"Cara, you know the rules. The only way to get me to stop is a veggie."

Hesitation drifted over her body until she moved as he'd instructed.

He slid her dress up her thighs. "Lift your bottom. I don't want to ruin your pretty dress."

She did as he instructed and felt the fabric of the seat beneath her ass.

His hands never left her body. He placed a tender kiss on her knee and slowly trailed a path closer to her core. "Coop. We shouldn't do this here."

"Yes, we should." He blew a hot breath against her skin without touching her where she wanted him most. "You know what will happen if you scream?"

His finger slid into her folds. "Are you going to scream?"

"I can't make any promises," she said, and his finger stilled inside of her.

"If we had a bed, I'd stuff your mouth so full of my cock that you wouldn't be able to scream."

Her channel spasmed and gushed with desire.

"Don't worry, Cara, we'll do that too."

He pulled the finger from inside her, and she was rewarded with what felt like his tongue. His hot breath against her skin made her moan as he devoured her. Colors of lights burst behind her closed eyes as she held him in place while trying to lift her hips to meet his mouth. Her head rested back on her shoulders as she bit her lip. She was so close to an orgasm that her thighs tightened against him. His tongue was replaced with his fingers, sliding in and out of her channel.

"I can't trust you to be quiet." His words were whispered against her lips before he claimed them. She tasted herself on his lips as he pressed on her bud. Her entire body was tight as the orgasm hit. He'd swallowed her scream as she went over the edge, only slowing when she sagged bonelessly in the chair. "Stay put."

His other hand trailed a path down her body and over her breast as she felt him again between her thighs. The soft slide of his tongue slid over her wet folds.

"Turnabout is fair play, Cooper."

"I'm counting on it," he said as something smooth swiped across her sensitive folds. "Stand up, Cara."

He helped her stand before removing the blindfold, giving her a first look around the secluded dining room. A table sat to the side of them filled with half-eaten food and the champagne she'd drunk. Her breathing slowed as he inched the hem of her dress back in place.

"Did you enjoy dinner?" he asked while cupping her cheek. "I did."

He kissed her again, giving her a taste of her juices. She reached between them, cupped his erection and rubbed it with her palm. "You surprised me, Coop. That's hard to do."

"The night's young, Cara. If you were surprised with this, I've got another one that will knock your socks off."

"You aren't going to take me to the swingers, are you? Because I have to draw the line somewhere."

"Nope. No swingers, just us. I promise."

She nodded as he led her to the door. She stopped him before opening it. "Do I look okay?"

"You look flushed." He winked.

She let out a relieved breath as he opened the door. Cooper held her hand as he led her through the restaurant. Her cheeks heated as she caught Phillip's gaze. His gaze followed them as they made their way along the restaurant wall toward the exit.

Cooper led her for a walk in the moonlight down the beach. They'd shared easy banter without the worries of their sisters. He'd told her about his work, and she'd talked about the work she did with her sisters. The energy in the air was charged, every fiber of her being keenly aware of how he touched her and every time he kissed her lips. His foreplay was killing her, and she'd found her release not once but twice. She could only imagine what it was doing to him.

Coop finally led her back toward the hotel, only stopping once more to kiss her beneath the canopy of trees. "I would insist on skinny-dipping, but I promised to wear condoms." He glanced at her. "I'm clean, though. You know, in case you change your mind."

Moisture gathered between her thighs. "I'm clean too. I'm just not on birth control. I hadn't had a need until...you."

Cooper's jaw clenched as if he was lost in thought as he glanced at the private pool as they turned into their room. He opened the door and ushered her inside, only letting go to lock the door. He stroked her arms and kissed her neck. She tilted her head to give him better access. "What now?"

She hadn't needed to ask. He slowly lowered the zipper of her dress. His warm palms touched her back as he eased them to her cup her breasts. The dress slid easily down her arms and pooled at her feet. She was naked from the waist down. Only her black lacy bra covered her breasts, and he had no problem unhooking it and divesting her of that too.

His hands skimmed up her waist to cradle her breasts, his thumbs flicking her nipples. Coop pressed tightly against her back, his hard cock trapped between them. The need to touch him consumed her every thought as he tweaked her nipples again, shooting a direct path to her wet core.

She wiggled her ass against him, hoping now was the time he'd ravish her. He released her breasts, stepping back to put an inch of space between them.

Coolness greeted her back. "You want more, don't you, Cara?"

His fingers trailed a slow path down her stomach between her folds. He slid a finger inside her. "You want me here?"

"Yes."

He released his hold. "Get on the bed."

The butterflies in her belly danced with delight as she climbed on top of the covers and held his gaze. She watched as he stripped his clothes, the shirt falling carelessly to the floor as he reached for the button on his pants. He'd stripped from head to toe in less than a minute, his eagerness fanning the flames of her desire. He was beautiful from the muscles of his tanned chest to the determination in his eyes. He was a man used to getting what he wanted, and he wanted her.

He stood at the end of the bed and stroked his erection, a bead of precum forming on the tip. "I've been waiting for this all night."

"Tell me you have condoms and not the ones my aunt gave you."

"Perks of the honeymoon suite." He moved to the bedside table and pulled out a box, tossing it onto the bed. He crawled up the mattress, settling between her thighs. Coop made a trail of kisses up her stomach, his lips making her burn, to her breast where he took it in his mouth, his tongue laving the hardened peak.

She held his head and arched her back, pressing closer to him. Sparks were shooting from her breasts throughout her body, every nerve ending lighting up.

He reached for the box of condoms, sliding one out, as he teased her nipple with his teeth before releasing it. He sat back on his legs and held her gaze while he made quick work of sheathing his length.

The scent of latex filled the air, and she felt her stomach clench in anticipation of what was to come.

"Do I need the safe word?" she asked as she lay back and smiled up at him.

"No. That playtime is over." He winked. "Although I do have some handcuffs in case you want to continue."

He rested his elbow next to her and used his other hand to slide his cock through her wet folds, teasing her until she wanted to beg. "How are you enjoying your one-night stand?"

"I'll enjoy it more when you quit teasing me."

He slid inside her, not stopping until he was seated to the hilt. The move took her breath away as he deliciously stretched her walls, making her feel more complete than she had ever felt before. "Is that better?"

"God yeah."

He took up a slow, easy rhythm of thrust and retreat, the friction from his cock giving her the best kind of chills. Cara scraped her nails down his back as his movement increased, the headboard banging into the wall with every stroke. He kissed her lips as he pounded into her, his thrusts getting harder and faster until she could barely catch her breath. Her walls clenched around him, grasping at his cock, her body wanting more.

"I'm not going to last this first time," he whispered into her hair. Cooper slowed his motion and leaned back, watching as he entered her. The desire in his eyes met hers, nearly taking her breath away. The want was evident on his hard, chiseled face. He reached between them, his fingers dancing over her clit as he quickened his pace. "That's it, baby."

Cara's eyes slid closed as her breath quickened. Her body tensed and strained for a release that remained just out of reach. She wanted to come so badly; her skin was hot and tight. "Coop," she said on a breath.

He lowered to press his body into hers and strummed her clit faster. "Look at me, Cara."

Her eyes slid opened as she met his gaze. "Are you ready?"

She raked her nails as her reply.

"Good. Come for me." He pressed down on her clit and took her hard and fast. Her walls clenched as her orgasm hit. His name echoed from her lips as he thrust a few more times until he found his own release. He stilled, buried deep inside of her. Despite the latex barrier, she could feel it when he found his release. His rapid breathing slowed as he stared deeply into her eyes.

His look had turned to one of confusion before he kissed her lips. He slowly slid out of her and rolled onto his side, pulling her into the crook of his arm. He glanced down at his cock. "Uh, I think the condom broke."

She should have been scared out of her wits. Worry should have clouded her mind, but the broken condom had been an accident. One that he could attest to. It wasn't like she'd end up pregnant. She'd been trying to get pregnant for years using every procedure known to man.

"I'm sure it's fine."

He pulled her into his chest. "If not, we'll deal with it. It was an accident, Cara. I would never do something like that on purpose."

"I know." She kissed his chest. "I think you've ruined me."

"How so?" he asked and kissed her forehead.

"Now I know what I'm missing with one-night stands." She glanced up at him as he cupped her cheek.

"Tonight." He shook his head as if he'd lost his train of thought. "That wasn't a typical one-night stand. One-night stands are just sex. This...this was more." He lay back down on the pillow.

Cara closed her eyes as the walls around her heart started to build again. He was wrong. This was a one-night stand. The only night they'd ever share, and she had only a few hours left to make it memorable for them both, so she did.

No more condom mishaps occurred, no words of love, no promises of commitment. Just pure unadulterated lust rolled through them both. Tomorrow she'd deal with the aftermath.

Chapter 11

Cara woke up in the darkness. The silence of the room was unnerving. Coop's arm was draped across her chest. The heavy feel of his touch would comfort anyone else, not Cara. Not in that moment. Something was wrong. She could feel it deep down into her bones.

Shadows danced across the ceiling, playing tricks on her mind as her heart raced.

"Coop," she whispered into the darkness.

Coop stirred. His hold on her tightened.

"Cooper," she said louder, with a little nudge.

He blinked his tired eyes open. "It's still dark out, Cara. Go back to sleep."

"Something's wrong," she whispered, afraid even mumbling the words would make them true.

Coop lifted his arm and ran his hand across his face. "What is it?"

"I don't know." She flicked the switch on the bedside lamp. The room was empty. She and Coop sat up in the bed. The covers lay at their waists. They both glanced around the room.

"Our stuff." Cara pointed to where their suitcases had once lain. The spot was now empty.

Coop slid his hand beneath his pillow and produced a gun she hadn't realized he'd hidden. He slipped from the bed. The barrel of the gun pointed at the ground. He was a vision, all six feet two of tanned nakedness, giving the word commando a dual meaning.

Cara lifted the covers to her chest and pulled them from the bed as she rose. She was afraid to breathe, afraid to move. Whoever had taken their things had to have done it while they'd slept. Fear coiled in her veins, tightening like a ball made from rubber bands about to burst.

"They were here when we got back, weren't they?" Cara asked as Cooper flicked on the light switch in the bathroom and yanked the shower curtain back.

"Yeah, and I had flipped the extra lock on the door."

He lowered his gun as he re-entered the room. His jaw clenched tightly as anger claimed the features on his face. He stalked to the front door and yanked it open, disappearing outside and then returning.

"Anything?"

"No." He let out a long breath. "Whoever was in here is gone."

Cara's body heated, and she clutched the sheet tighter. "Coop. You know what this means?"

Coop ran his hand over his neck. "Yep. Someone was in here when we got back from dinner."

"Oh my God." Her hand flew to cover her mouth. "They were in here when we..."

Coop stormed to the phone and picked up the receiver. He punched in some numbers and demanded security before slamming the phone back in place.

"You realize we're both naked? No clothes and you're going to let them in here?"

Coop grabbed the blanket from the bed and wrapped her into it like a guy wrapping a Christmas present. He told her to hold one end and twirl into him, cocooning her into the fabric. She was two seconds away from busting free. Not because of the confining weight, but from her temper, which was about to burst free.

Some no-good, low-life, son of a bitch had been in their room and witnessed everything. Every moan, every scream, every smack of their bodies as they'd had sex. Coop wasn't going to need a gun if he found the bastard. She'd scratch out his eyes and tear off his ears to undo what he'd stolen.

She struggled against the heavy weight as he disappeared into the bathroom and walked out, with a beach towel covering the important parts that she'd gotten to know extremely well only hours before. Cara wobbled to the bedside phone. She struggled to free her arm and lifted the receiver. There was only one person on the island that could help her. She dialed the front desk. "Connect me to room 259."

Coop held the door open for Phillip to enter with two guards trailing behind him. Phillip held her gaze as Cara spoke into the phone.

"Hi, Aunt Betty, it's Cara. I need a favor. I need you to bring me some clothes. We're in the honeymoon cabana."

"What happened to your clothes, Cara?"

Cara turned away from the crowd and lowered her voice. "We were robbed. They took everything. Can you stop by the gift shop and get something for Coop to wear too?"

"Sure. What size is he?"

Cara covered the phone. "Coop, what size do you wear?"

"Thirty-six long."

"He's a thirty-six long. We need everything. We're both naked as the day we were born."

Aunt Betty's laughter rang out, and Cara held the phone away from her ear.

"This isn't funny, Aunt Betty. Someone violated us."

"I know. I'm sorry. Please tell me you at least got some of his swimmers."

Cara clenched her eyes closed, tightening the grip of the phone in her hand. "It's not like that. Just come and hurry." Cara glanced over her shoulder. "There are security men in the room. I'm not sure how much more I can handle before I really lose my shit."

"Okay, okay, give me ten minutes."

"Thank you," Cara whispered and hung up the phone.

Cara lumbered out the front door and plopped down in a patio chair. The ocean breeze did little to cool her heated skin. Her mind raced as she remembered everything they'd done in the room.

"I want footage from every camera within a mile of this room, and I want it ready for my review." Cooper's voice rose as he spoke. "I don't care if I have to search every damn inch of your hotel. You can bet your ass I'm going to find out who's responsible."

"Agent Cruz, we're doing the best we can."

"It's not good enough. Call the police and get their forensic team out here. I want the entire room dusted for prints." His angry voice grew louder before he stomped outside and squeezed his neck.

She'd expected to wake up and deal with awkward, but nothing could have prepared her for this. Calming words eluded her. She was of no help to him. They'd get through this like everything else.

"Cara, we're going to find this guy." He meant what he said. She could hear the conviction in his voice.

"I know." She rose, shifting the blanket. "I'm going to help, just like I found the missing speaker."

"No." Coop's jaw ticked. "Touching people wears you out, and there are God knows how many people here, including those swingers. Do you really want to see what they've been up to?"

"Coop," she said as she approached him. "We might not have a choice if the security cameras are still down." She gestured to the room. "We might get lucky and get prints, but if the police haven't found this person yet, chances are he's not leaving any evidence behind."

Coop rested his palms on where her shoulders would be if she wasn't swaddled in the blanket. "It's just clothing, Cara. Tomorrow you go back with Aunt Betty, and I'll stay and catch this guy."

"It's more than that, Coop." She held his gaze. "That person violated me. Violated us. I can't just walk away when I can help you catch him."

"She's right, and you know it, Cruz," Aunt Betty announced as she approached. She tossed Coop one of the bags she was carrying and handed Cara the other. "Cara, go get dressed while I talk to Cruz."

Coop dug through the bag and pulled a bathing suit from the bag. He ripped the tag off. "I'll pay you back for this."

"Don't worry about it."

Coop turned around, slid the shorts beneath his towel, and buttoned it before dropping the towel on the table. He sorted through the shirts and picked one of the flowered shirts that looked like it had been designed for an eighty-year-old. Beggars couldn't be choosers, and right now, he had squat. Neither of them did.

"It's true that touching people zaps her energy. Her ability can be a pain in the ass, not to mention making her lonely, but you already knew that."

Betty raised a brow in challenge.

Coop crossed his arms over his chest. "You know she can't read me."

"I know." Aunt Betty smiled. "You two needed each other more than you even realized."

"So you've said." He dropped his arms to his side.

"Cara's a Thornton. We never take the easy route. It's encoded in our DNA. It was better letting her figure it out on her own. I just gave her a little shove to send her into your chaos."

Coop ran his hand over his head. "She kicked me out of her office."

Betty patted his shoulder. "You aren't the first, and I'm sure you won't be the last. But just like she could help you then, she can help you now. She's not afraid of her gift. She just chooses to avoid using it, but when she uses it wisely, she can accomplish more."

"And how do you suppose I do that?" Cara asked, walking out of the cabana in Daisy Duke short shorts and a tank top that hugged every one of her curves. Thank God for Aunt Betty.

Phillip followed behind Cara, interrupting their conversation. "I've called it in and the forensic team will be here in just a bit. It might be a good idea if you two steer clear of the crime scene. Call your banks or whatever you have to do, cancel any credit cards and deal with the missing items. Of course, the resort will work with you to replace what you need for the remainder of your stay."

"Thanks for your help." Cooper shook Phillip's hand. Phillip smiled at Cara and gave a little nod of his head.

Phillip cleared his throat and held Cara's gaze. "Cara, can I speak to you privately."

Privately? Cara had the deer in the headlights look as she held Coop's gaze. "Uh, sure."

Phillip gestured toward the beach and waited for Cara to lead the way. Coop should have stopped her. Phillip shouldn't have anything to say to her that he couldn't say in front of the others. Coop started to follow, but Betty grabbed his arm and shook her head. "She can handle herself. You're both just pretending, remember?"

Knots twisted in Cooper's gut as he watched Phillip and Cara stroll toward the water's edge.

Chapter 12

"I'm sorry all of this happened to you, and on your honeymoon." Phillip held her gaze. Sincerity registered on his face.

"It's not your fault." She gave him a sad smile.

"Seeing you again, after all these years, was a shock. Seeing how smart and beautiful you are...I wish we would have stayed in touch."

Wasn't that how every man thought when seeing an old fling with another man? Did her marital status, even fake, make her more appealing? He could have reached out. He could have returned her calls all those years ago. She pushed the thoughts from her head. Men like Phillip realized a good thing only when it was gone. Would Coop be the same way?

"That was a long time ago. People change and grow up. I'm glad to see you're doing well. Was there something you wanted to talk about?" Cara asked, glancing up to the cabana where Coop was talking to Aunt Betty.

"I don't want to start any trouble between you and him, but I just wanted to tell you." Phillip's gaze bore into hers. "If things don't work out, not that I wish you two ill, but you know, if you ever find yourself available or just need someone to talk to, I'm here."

Was he serious? Cara's mouth parted as she stared up at Phillip in disbelief. Talk about rude. Cooper would rip this guy a new asshole if she and he'd really been married. It was one thing to have a past, but he might as well have just come out and said that he was standing by as an option when things went south. Cara snapped her mouth closed and crossed her arms over her chest. "I can't believe you just said that to me."

Phillip held up his hands in surrender. "I didn't mean any disrespect."

"I'm not sure Coop will see it that way. What makes you think he and I won't last?"

Phillip's brows dipped. "It doesn't take a genius to come to that conclusion. You two couldn't be more opposite, Cara. He's all business and you're not. You're a free spirit, at least you used to be. You saw things with your heart. That guy can't possibly appreciate you, or respect what you have to offer."

"I'm not the same girl I was when I was eighteen, and you don't know him." Cara balled her fists and planted them on her hips. His every word pushed her to the boiling point, until she thought she might explode.

Phillip pulled his phone from his pocket, hit a few buttons, turned it to face her. "Does this look like a man that values you?"

Cara watched the video. She didn't need to hear the audio for the memories to come crashing back. She was on a chair in the private dining room, a blindfold around her eyes, and Cooper's head was between her thighs. Cara's heart somersaulted into her stomach as bile rose in her throat. This wasn't happening. "Where did you get that?"

"I was in the security office when it happened, but don't worry. I only recorded some so I could show you, but I deleted the original. No one but I saw what was happening. You're lucky it was only me, Cara. If he cared, how could he put you in that predicament without being absolutely sure that you wouldn't get hurt?"

Cara crossed her arm around her waist. She felt exposed, and it had nothing to do with the skimpy outfit she was wearing.

Phillip ran his hands over his face. "Listen, I'm sorry it had to come out this way. Just..." He shoved his hands in his pocket. "Just know if you need me, I'll be there. It doesn't matter why or when. I'll just be there."

"Are you going to delete that?" She gestured to his phone.

He clicked a few buttons and turned an empty screen back to her. "Done. Just be careful, okay?"

"Thank you." Cara turned and walked away. She had no destination in mind as she followed the wet sand. All she knew was she needed to calm down before she talked to Coop. She was partially to blame for what had happened between them. She'd been eager for his touch, for the rush that had consumed her from the compromising position. He couldn't have known there was a camera. He had to have been smarter than that.

Cara wasn't the kind of woman to go running from her problems. She wasn't the type to not take responsibility for her actions. It wasn't as if the video would send her into hiding or hating Coop, but she'd be hard-pressed to trust that it wouldn't happen again. Cara ended up in a hidden alcove. She sat on one the rocks with her feet buried in the wet sand as she watched the sun start to peek over the horizon. The vibrant orange and yellow hues did nothing to chase away her thoughts. She had no idea how much time had passed as she sat lost in thought. Coop was a good man. He wouldn't have intentionally hurt her. Deep down she knew she was right.

"There you are," Coop called out as he rounded the rocks that hid her from the beach-goers. "The forensic team is in our room. What are you doing way down here?" Coop asked, coming to stand between her legs and laying a gentle hand on her thigh.

"I...um...I just needed a bit of time to process. That's all."

Coop used his finger to lift her chin so she could look at him. "Everything will be okay. This thief messed up. He stole federal property when he stole my wallet with my badge inside. I just got off the phone with my partner, and he's on his way to help find this creep."

"That's great." She gave him a smile she knew didn't reach her eyes. She couldn't muster more enthusiasm. Her heart ached as she looked into Coop's eyes. Every good thing eventually has to end.

"What did Phillip want to talk about?" Coop asked, as if he knew her talk with Phillip had something to do with how she was acting.

"He..." She cleared her throat. "He wanted to tell me that there was a video of us in the private dining room. He wanted to reassure me that he deleted it and no one else saw it."

"That's not possible." Coop shook his head. "I specifically asked when I made the arrangements, and after I blindfolded you, I made sure there were no cameras hanging from the walls."

Cara placed her hand over his and squeezed. "It's okay, Coop. I don't blame you. I could have stopped you, but I didn't. I wanted that to happen as much as you, if not more."

Coop cupped her cheek, and his face softened. "It's not okay."

She placed her palm over his. "What are we doing, Coop? This isn't you; it isn't me. You're like an addiction that's going to be hard for me to kick when we get back to reality."

"One problem at a time, Cara." He lowered his lips and pressed a tender kiss to her mouth. "Let's go check out those cameras and buy some new things."

Laughter bubbled from her lips. "Yeah? How are we going to do that?

Neither one of us has any cash or credit cards."

He lifted her off the rock. Her body slid slowly down his before he entwined their fingers together and started back up the beach. "There's a lot you don't know about me, Cara. You thought you knew who I was because of my last name, but honey, you have no idea."

She was beginning to realize that. "Enlighten me; how do you plan to pay for stuff when neither of us has a dime. I'm allergic to washing dishes."

"You didn't find it odd that your Aunt Betty sent you to my house that night with a diaper bag? How do you think she knew I needed one?"

Cara didn't know what to believe anymore. "I never thought to ask."

Coop glanced at her. His eyes twinkled in the sunlight. "She sent the diaper bag and you because she knew I was in over my head." He squeezed her fingers. "She knew I was in over my head because she's known me for a long time. I was assigned as her partner after the academy. When she told me she was retiring to open a bar, I decided to invest as a silent partner. I own half of the bar. I figured it would be a nice distraction when I retire."

Cara's mouth parted before she snapped it closed. How had she not known that Aunt Betty was in business with a

Cruz? After she'd witnessed the tears and the betrayal. How come she hadn't come clean? Maybe that was why she hadn't come clean. "I didn't know."

"Now you do. So being as my business partner just happens to be on the island, she'll foot the bill for everything and anything we need. I'll pay her back. She knows I'm good for it. Not to mention, you're her niece. She wouldn't have left you stranded."

Coop led Cara into the hotel boutique. They had an array of clothes, only most of them were geared toward an older crowd. Not that she minded changing out of her aunt's Daisy Dukes. Still. She passed on the large flowered dresses that would swallow her whole, opting instead for a few items that looked like they were meant to flow. Whoever had stolen their clothes was a perv, not even leaving their underwear behind. Bastard.

They'd both changed into clothes they could wear into the restaurant before he pulled her through it. The smell of bacon, sausage, and pancakes had her mouthwatering as he led her into the private dining room. He paused inside the empty room. The table from the night before was pushed against the wall. The place had been cleaned. Her gaze traveled the length of the walls. Coop was right.

There hadn't been any video cameras in sight. How exactly had Phillip seen it?

Coop grabbed one of the chairs and placed it where she'd sat last night. "What angle was the video coming from?"

Cara sat down in the chair, remembering the angle from the shot. She pointed toward one of the walls where a plant was hung.

Coop grabbed another chair, walked over to the wall, stood on top of it. He dug around inside the plastic plant.

"Sir, guests aren't allowed to stand on the furniture," one of the workers said.

He jumped down and looked behind the plant. He ran his fingers along the wall. A smile slipped on his lips. "What's behind this wall?"

"Uh...the kitchen. Well directly behind the wall where you're standing is the supply room and then the kitchen."

"Take us there," Coop demanded and took Cara's hand.

"Sir, guests aren't allowed in the kitchen."

"Ma'am, I'm Special Agent Cruz with the FBI, and if you don't take me to the supply closet, I'll have your ass arrested for interfering with a federal investigation."

"Coop, this doesn't have anything to do with the thefts," Cara whispered.

"It could." He winked. "For all we know, that could be where the thief is stashing the goods."

Cara placed a smile on her face as she turned to the woman. "Please, let us see the supply closet. We won't take long, and we promise to leave your name out if anyone gets upset."

The woman nodded. "Come with me. I'll bring you in the back way so my manager and the other guests won't see."

"There's a back way?" Coop asked as we crossed the empty room.

"Of course. The hotel has a lot of back entrances that are for employees only. Kind of an out of sight, out of mind thing. The management didn't want housekeepers and such being in the guests' way. So we all use the back entrances."

The woman swiped her card key into the security lock, making the door buzz open. Cara and Coop followed behind her as she stopped at another door and swiped it again. She stepped back and let Coop and Cara enter the dark room.

Coop flipped a switch, and a low light illuminated their surroundings. Boxes filled the room labeled napkins and condiments, and there were a few empty hotel bags that were distributed to the guests' rooms for dirty clothes. Cara peered in one as Coop moved to the adjoining wall, about where the plant from the adjoining dining room would be hung. He shoved some boxes aside and grinned.

"Ma'am, do you have a cell phone?"

"Sure." She pulled it out and handed it to him.

Coop took a picture before his fingers flew across the screen. He handed it back to her. "Don't delete that picture until you're told by either Agent Howard Stallman or me. He's en route. I emailed it to him for safekeeping."

She nodded and shoved the phone back into her apron.

"Cara, hand me one of those plastic hotel bags."

Cara handed it to him. Coop used the bag to scoop up something near his feet without touching it with his hands.

"What did you find?"

"Evidence."

He grabbed another bag, picked up a few more items, and placed them in the bag. Her wallet and his, their phones, along with the black satin bra she'd worn the night before, were among the items.

"Oh my God."

"I know."

"Coop, you realize who did this? He deleted the video. We won't be able to prove it."

"We'll prove it." He smiled and moved out of the room, taking her hand. He pulled the door closed.

"Ma'am, I'm going to have to ask you not to tell anyone that we were in here. Do you understand?"

"Of course. You might want to hurry, though. We have a shift change in thirty minutes."

"Which is the fastest way out without us running into anyone?"

"Follow me."

Chapter 13

Hours later, Cara was in the shower as Coop spoke to his friend and co-worker. Agent Howard Stillman had been his new partner since Betty had decided to retire. The man was like a brother to Coop.

"He filmed us."

"Filmed you doing what?"

"He filmed us in a compromising position. He showed her the video and claimed that it was caught on a security camera. Looks like he enjoyed himself." Coop handed over the plastic bag containing the used and dirty dishtowel that he'd found on the ground, near the hole in the wall.

"Sick fuck." Howard grabbed the bag. "We'll get his DNA off this."

"You need to move fast. If he knows we were in that room, there's a chance he'll destroy his phone, especially if he's aware that we can retrieve the deleted video. They've had a rash of robberies. There are corridors that the staff uses to move through the building undetected. When you arrest him, make sure you check out the tunnels. If I had to guess, either one of the staff or he is using them to smuggle out the stolen stuff."

"I'll handle it." Howard gestured toward the cabana. "So is that the girl? Did you really tie the knot, like Betty saw in her vision?"

"That's her, but she doesn't know that Betty told me about the vision. If she knew her aunt even had the vision, she'd be pissed that I had purposefully avoided her for the last six months."

"I think she'd be more pissed that you were the reason your brother broke things off with her."

"What?" Cara's anger was palpable, in the tremor that racked her body and the way her eyes slit at him. Her cell phone was clutched in her hand, and she looked like she wanted to launch it at him like a weapon. "You what!"

"Time to come clean, man. I'm sorry." Howard patted him on the back as he headed out into the path of trees.

"Answer me, damn it. Aunt Betty had a vision about us; she told you, and then you avoided me? Is it true?"

"Cara, I can explain."

Cara held up her hand to stop him from stepping toward her. "You knew all this time, and you avoided me." A tear slipped down her face, but it wasn't an upset tear. It looked more like an I'm-fucking-pissed-off tear. "And Eric? You're the reason we broke up?"

"Hey, I just suggested it when I told him about the vision. I didn't tell him to go sleep with your best friend."

"I can't..." She stormed over to him. "Squash," she screamed as she shoved him backward into the pool and began to run. He'd known all this time. He'd been the one responsible for her heartache, and yet he'd never said anything. Neither had Aunt Betty. Her own flesh and blood. Tears streamed down Cara's face.

Cara hurried through the canopy of trees that cloaked her from the moon above. She heard a branch break from behind her and turned when a hand reached out and grabbed her, covering her mouth. Beefy fingers dug into her cheek, bruising her tender flesh. Visions fought to take hold. She used her energy to hold them back. There was no way in hell she was blacking out.

Terror traveled down her spine and bile rose in her throat as she fought to get free before the hard metal of a gun pressed against her temple. An eerie calm settled over her as she pressed the recorder button on her phone, knowing its location by heart because of the readings that she recorded.

"Cara," Coop hollered out as the pounding of his feet passed where they stood. Her assailant inched her around the base of a tree, keeping her from being seen, the shadows swallowing their bodies.

"Don't move or I'll kill him," a voice she knew all too well whispered in her ear. Phillip.

Her body froze on the spot as ice traveled down her spine. He'd been the one with the video. She'd known that. She'd known he'd been the one spying, but knowing, and being in his clutches, replaced her anger with fear.

"Let me go," she mumbled beneath his hand. Every time she blinked, she'd get pieces of visions that were seeping through, the flickering images making a headache build behind her eyes.

"You're a slut. You haven't changed a bit. You were one when you were eighteen, and you still are. Do you know what I like to do with women like you?"

Tears streamed down her face as she shook her head, afraid of what he might say. Her hands clenched at her sides, wanting to claw at the man holding her hostage.

"I'm going to cut you up, to the point that any man who sees you will be disgusted. Cooper won't want anything to do with you, and then maybe he'll see I did him a favor. Then I'm going to cuff him to the bed and fuck him like he wanted to do to you. You did me a favor all those years ago. It's because of you that I realized I liked men, and not just any men, but the ones that fight back. I bet Special Agent Cruz is a fighter. I can't wait to find out."

Cara had to swallow the bile rising in her throat. Cruz would be blindsided. Cara clenched her eyes closed and then lost against the visions she'd been fighting to hold back. They flooded her senses, bombarding her, back to back.

Phillip with one man after another handcuffed to a bed as he had sex with each. Some were familiar, and others weren't. One was the missing speaker that she'd found. His back had cuts and was bleeding. His body slumped against the bed as Phillip pounded into him. "Oh God, no."

"You're seeing it, aren't you?" Phillip's hold on her tightened. "How I take them and break them before killing them and turning them into fish food. It's going to be worse for your husband, and the best part...I'm going to make you watch."

More visions assaulted her. Phillip entering in and out of rooms, laughing as he stole items from several guests. Another of Phillip, only younger, the way he'd looked when they first met. He was inside a bar where male strippers danced on the stage.

Cara tossed her phone into the grass to distract him as she struggled against his hold. The butt of the gun came down on her temple, making the visions disappear. Her last thought was of Cooper as she slipped out of consciousness.

Coop ran into the hotel, leaving a path of water as he ignored the looks the other guests gave him. Howard was standing at the concierge desk when Coop approached.

"She came this way. Where is she?" Coop asked, his gaze searching the lobby.

"She didn't come this way, Coop. I've been in the lobby getting the information on Phillip since I left you. She hasn't been in here."

"Fuck." Coop ran his hand through his wet hair. "She came this way. I saw which way she turned out of the cabana as she ran."

"I'll help you find her." Howard glanced back at the concierge. "Call the local PD and tell them to put out an all-points bulletin on Cara Thornton and Phillip. Consider him armed and dangerous. Have the remainder of your security team keep their eyes peeled, and have them search room by room for Mrs. Thornton. Tell the local PD to form a search party. Give them my number if they give you any lip." Howard slid a card across the desk.

The concierge nodded as the blood drained from his face.

"Do it now," Coop demanded when the guy was slow to pick up the phone.

Coop hurried out of the hotel with Howard, and they checked each and every pool cabana as they passed, systematically clearing each inch as they hit the tree line. They were checking the canopy of trees and around each one when Coop felt something beneath his foot. He picked it up. The screen on it showed that someone had been recording something.

Coop hit Play and listened in horror as Phillip threatened her. His heart clenched as he listened, word for word, to what the sick fuck wanted to do to them both. "Oh, I'll kill you first, you sick fuck."

Cooper stepped back onto the sidewalk and held up the phone for Howard to see. "He's got her."

The old couple, Coop and Cara had breakfast with their first morning, came strolling down the path. Both of them shared a worried look as they neared. "Dear, is your wife okay? John and I were talking a stroll down the beach and admiring one of the houses for sale when we saw that hotel security guard carrying her inside. Is there anything we can do?"

Howard and Coop exchanged a look. "Which house was it? There are three that I noticed for sale."

"The one with the yellow shutters. That's why I liked the house, although this tightwad won't agree to let me have it."

Coop kissed the lady on the forehead in his excitement and was about to take off when Howard grabbed his arm.

"Be smart. You can't go busting in there like Rambo. It will get her killed. We do this the right way and you both walk out alive."

Chapter 14

Cara kept her eyes closed and her body limp, using her senses. She lay on a hard wooden floor, the cold seeping through her clothes to chill her body. Her wrists were restrained, the bindings digging into her tender skin, but she felt nothing at her feet. The room reeked of mold and mildew, a place that obviously hadn't been cleaned in a while. Yet she could hear the sounds of the waves crashing against the shore. She was still on the island, and even better, near the beach. She could find her way back to Coop, if she could just get out of this. All she needed was for him to make one wrong move and she'd escape.

She peeked through her eyelashes, not ready to let on that she was conscious.

The room was dark. The only light was from the moonlight peeking through the windows, casting a glow on the hard floor.

"I know you're awake." Phillip's voice drifted to her ears. "I can tell by your breathing."

His heavy footsteps neared, and black combat boots appeared in her vision. Material crinkled, and she opened her eyes to find that he'd squatted in front of her. Phillip ran the cold, hard barrel of the gun down her tear-stained cheek, eliciting a shiver down her body. She struggled against her binds.

"He's going to find you, and he's going to kill you." She spat the words into his face.

He swiped it away and shoved the gun into her chest. "Not before I'm finished with you." He ripped open her shirt and ran the gun between her breasts. The metal was cold on her skin and her chest heaved.

I'm going to die. The gun lowered over her stomach, where he shoved the barrel into her belly button.

"He should have been more careful with the condom." Phillip looked at her with cold-blooded eyes as a sneer lifted his lips. He slipped a knife from his pocket and flicked it open. Moving the knife over the exact spot the gun had just been. The sharp blade pressed against her stomach, making her afraid to move, afraid to breathe.

The sharp end pressed deeper into her skin. A trickle of blood ran over her abdomen. Anger and fear drained her hope to escape.

"Please don't. I'm begging you," she whispered.

His smile grew, and he licked his lips as the knife moved up her body, stopping at her chest. He leaned into her and licked a path up her cheek.

"I'm not going to kill you....yet." He slammed the knife into the skin above her breast. She screamed. The pain seared through her like a red-hot poker. Dots claimed her vision as he pulled the knife free.

Cara's tear-filled eyes narrowed, and she did the only thing she could. She smashed her forehead against his. The move sent him reeling onto his ass and made stars dance in her eyes. The gun he'd once held flew beneath a coffee table, the knife just out of reach. She scrambled for it and got to her feet, holding the knife in front of her bound hands, using it as a shield.

Phillip stilled on the ground, and his hands roamed the floor around him, probably in search of his gun. "You won't get far, Cara, and when I find you, I'm going to fill you full of holes. You won't live to disgust anyone else."

Phillip dropped his gaze and frantically looked for the gun. Cara turned and ran. The door was locked and bolted into place. She glanced over her shoulder to find that Phillip was reaching for the gun.

Her heart raced as she took off for the stairs, trying to put as much distance between a bullet and herself as she could. There were only two doors at the top of the stairs, both open; one was a bathroom and the other a bedroom. She hurried into the bedroom and slammed the door closed, twisting the lock. Her gaze ran over the bedroom furniture. Under the bed would have her trapped and unable to fight back. The window was partially open. She didn't have time to cut through her bonds and climb out the window. She was stuck with nowhere to go, and only a knife to keep her alive.

She moved into the closet and stepped inside the darkened space, easing the door shut.

"Cara," Phillip called out. "There's nowhere to run."

Tears streamed down her face as her body trembled. Goosebumps covered her arms as a hand appeared from nowhere and covered her mouth. A hard, familiar body pressed against her back.

"I've got you," Coop whispered in her ear and lifted his hand.

"Why were you in the closet?"

"I wanted to have the element of surprise. I heard someone running upstairs." He took the knife and sliced through the rope around her wrists and moved her body behind him.

Relief flooded her system as Cooper aimed his gun at the closed door.

"How did you find me?" She couldn't stop the trembles in her fingers as she held on to his hip on one side while holding the knife in her other hand.

"Luck," he answered.

"I know you're in here," Phillip called out.

Coop held the gun with both hands and aimed it at the door.

The knob of the closet door turned, making Cara gasp.

"I can hear you," Phillip spoke as the door swung open.

Coop pulled the trigger.

He never missed a target. One bullet through the head. Phillip was lying broken and dead on the floor as Coop pulled Cara against his chest and eased her out of the room and over the body. He sat her on the bed and clicked the comm in his ear. "I've got her. Second floor. She's hurt. Call EMS and the coroner's office."

Howard came bursting through the door with a phone pressed against his ear. "We need an ambulance. Female, age thirty-two, looks like a knife wound to the chest." Howard glanced to the opposite side of the room. "The assailant is dead."

Howard shook his head. "No, I don't know the address. Shit." Howard cursed as he left the room.

Coop pulled the shirt over his head and sat next to her, pressing the fabric into her wound. She looked dazed, as if the pressure and pain were making the room spin around her.

"Cara, stay with me."

She shook her head as her eyes slipped closed.

Coop carried Cara, cradled against his chest, down the stairs, refusing to lay her down. He held her until the ambulance arrived and carried her inside, placing her on the gurney.

He kept touching her, afraid if he stopped and she woke, she'd get visions of the paramedics working to access the damage. The paramedics were asking him questions about allergies and her medical history, none of which he knew. When they asked if she might be pregnant, that question made him pause. "Possibly."

He'd never considered having children, maybe because he'd never met the right woman. Coop's gaze caressed Cara. Coop had caused his own damage to her that needed repair. One problem at a time.

Chapter 15

Cara kept her gaze focused out the window the entire plane ride back to Florida, ignoring her Aunt Betty. Cooper had stayed on the island, to help settle the chaos that had ensued, and to give statements. Cara didn't care. Her body was numb, her heart unfeeling. It was surreal. Everything she'd experienced, everything she'd learned.

"Cara, don't be mad at Coop. Give him a chance to explain."

Cara turned toward her aunt. "There's nothing to explain. You knew; he knew, and neither one of you told me."

Cara turned back to the window and got lost in the haze of the clouds. She closed her eyes, hoping that Aunt Betty would take the hint. She did. For once in her life, she did. There were no witty remarks, no trying to make things right. Cara let the silence consume her until the plane jolted as the wheels met the tarmac.

The limo her father sent greeted the plane, and the ride to her mother's was quick. It was the last place she'd wanted to go, but she needed her car.

Coop's sister, Angela, was waiting on the porch with Cara's mother and sisters. Cara took a deep breath before getting out of the car.

None of them rushed to her side. They stood stoic, as if afraid to move.

"Cara," her mother said, stepping off the stairs. "We have something to tell you."

Her words made Cara pause. "Can it wait, Mom?"

"No, dear. It can't." Her mom guided Cara to stand in front of the others. "Tell her."

"Tell me what?" Cara asked.

"We lied," Harper said, sitting on the steps. The others followed and sat down too.

"All of us," Becca amended.

Aunt Betty moved to stand beside Cara. "It's my fault. I dragged them into it. If you're going to be angry, be angry at me."

Cara's heart clenched. The need to know ate at her gut.

"I was never in danger," Angela spoke.

"Technically, I did have a vision, but it wasn't Angela. It was about her brother and you," Becca amended.

"We couldn't come up with any other plan for you guys to work together."

"He loves me. I was the logical choice," Angela said.

"I called the plane home," her mom said, moving to stand next to the girls. "So you two wouldn't come rushing back."

"And you?" Cara asked, looking at Harper. "What did you do?"

"I didn't do anything." Harper held up her hands.

"You didn't tell me the truth." Anger stirred in Cara's body, awakening her suppressed emotions, letting the dam break free. "I've spent three days with a man that knew about me and didn't want me. I fucking slept with him. I could be pregnant. We both almost died, and all of you..." She gestured to the group. "All of you viewed this as some sick, twisted, fucking game."

A hot, angry tear slid down her face. Cara didn't wait for them to answer as she stormed to her car and yanked the door open. She slid behind the wheel, turned the key in the ignition and hit the gas. Where did the betrayal end?

Cara arrived home to find Ian greeting her at the door. He held his arms open, and she walked straight into his embrace as she finally let the tears she'd been holding back consume her. She braced herself for the visions, blocking what she could, and yet still, a few slipped by. It didn't matter. She didn't matter.

"Tell me you weren't in on it," she said through her sobs. "Tell me that you didn't know."

"Harper called and said you were upset. That's all I know." He cupped her cheek and glanced down at her. "I hate to see a lass cry. Tell me what happened, and I'll fix it."

Cara spent the next hour explaining how everything had gone wrong, and how the people she loved most had betrayed her trust. Ian ground his teeth as he paced the living room. He looked as angry as Cara had once felt. "Pack a bag, get your passport. You're leaving with me."

"I can't just go." Cara stood and clutched the blanket that had been covering her legs. "I have responsibilities."

Ian cupped her shoulders. "You have a responsibility to yourself, Cara. Let them deal with the aftermath. I'm sending you to Quinn on my private jet. She'll know what to do and how to make things right."

Cara's heart clutched as she chewed her lip. Quinn would know exactly what to do. She'd been through worse. Cara nodded. "Okay. I'll go see Quinn."

And she did. Within twenty-four hours, Cara had her head in her big sister's lap as Quinn stroked her hair, promising everything would be all right. Collin had walked into the room to find them in that position and slowly backed out, calling down the hall as he left, "Have Mavis make triple the brownies."

Coop, with a phone pressed to his ear, paced the living room and glared at Angela as she bounced Adam in her lap. Cara's voice mail picked up, and again and again, he left messages. Six weeks had passed, and still no one knew where she'd gone. Six fucking weeks he'd been out of his mind.

He disconnected the call and tossed his phone down on the table. Resting his fists on his hips, he narrowed his eyes at Eric. "Were you in on this?"

Eric held up his hands and rose from his seated position. "Hell no. No one told me, or I would have told you. The last thing this family needs is a kid with abilities. Cara's always wanted a baby. She even talked about freezing her eggs.

Knowing her, she probably tampered with the condom herself."

Coop lunged for his brother and slammed his fist into Eric's cheek. They grappled on the floor, each getting a good shot into the other, only stopping when Adam started to cry. "She's not like that. Take it fucking back."

Eric pushed off the floor and righted his shirt. He turned to Angela. "See, I told you he loves her. Even if the stubborn ass won't admit it to us."

"There's a difference between loving her and caring about her." Coop smacked his brother on the back of his head. He didn't love her, did he? Cared about her, absolutely, but love? He shoved the thought away when someone rang his doorbell. Hope blossomed in his chest that it was Cara.

He yanked the door open to find the Scot who had been staying at Cara's standing on his porch, wearing a kilt and holding an envelope.

"Ian McDougall, right? You were staying with Cara? Where is she?" Coop demanded.

"Nowhere any of you will get to her," Ian said, pushing around him and entering the house. "You're Cooper?" He glanced around at the others. "Angela and Eric?"

They all nodded.

"Where is she?" Coop asked.

Ian shoved the envelope against his chest. "Sign this."

"What is it?" Cooper asked, tearing into the envelope. He pulled out a document. "Termination of Parental Rights" was scrolled across the top. "I'm not signing this."

Ian crossed his arms over his chest and tilted his head. "She said you'd say that."

"I'm going to give her and her child a life filled with love and honor in Scotland, which is more than you're willing to offer. Sign the document."

Cooper tore the document in half and tossed it at Ian's feet. "I'm not signing that."

Ian's lips twitched. "She said you'd do that too."

It was a case of déjà vu. Hadn't he used those exact words on her the first time he'd entered Cara's office?

"I'm no' telling you where she is." Ian raised a brow in challenge.

"No need," Coop said. After grabbing his jacket, wallet, and his passport, he headed for the door.

KATE ALLENTON

Chapter 16

Quinn stood, by the edge of the cliffs, with her cell phone pressed against her ear.

"The package was delivered," Ian said across the line. "He refused and is on his way. He'll be about twelve hours behind the others. How's the little momma?"

"Ian, she's six weeks. She's fine except a little morning sickness."

"Aye." Ian's Scottish drawl was thick. "I'll be staying a wee bit. Let me know if there's anything else I need to do."

"Thanks for your help, Ian. Cara isn't going to be happy, but she'll get over it."

"Tell her my offer still stands. I'll raise the bairn and marry her."

Quinn rolled her eyes. Cara had refused the first five times Ian had asked. She wasn't about to change her mind. "What are you running from, McDougall, that you'd marry a woman you don't love?"

"A McDougall never runs, Lady Menzie. Call me if you need me."

"Aye," Quinn answered back. She had a million things to do and a short time to get them done.

Six hours later, Quinn stood in the study with her mother, her aunt Betty, and all of her sisters except Cara. She'd been resting late into the afternoon.

"I have to admit. You guys screwed up pretty darn bad. One might even say that this one screw-up trumps all of mine."

"Quinn, just tell me where she is," her mom said, sitting on the couch, her hands clenched together. "She won't return any of our calls, and I need to know she's okay."

"You should have thought about that, Mom." Quinn clasped her hands together. "You each have single-handedly destroyed her trust. She thought she was helping save her sister." Quinn stared at Becca. "Instead, she's been manipulated by the lot of you. She's been humiliated by finding out Cooper knew about her, and the visions, yet didn't want anything to do with her." Quinn's gaze turned to Aunt Betty. "She almost died. I can't say I really blame her for shutting you all out." Quinn lifted her hand to her chest. "I, on the other hand, am the good sister. I wasn't involved. I'm just cleaning up the mess."

Quinn chuckled. The words felt foreign on her tongue. "I've talked her off the ledge. I've eased her worries, and convinced her that you guys didn't deliberately set out to hurt her. That your lies came from a place of love."

"Yeah, that's you." Harper leaned back and crossed her legs. "All love and light. Tell me she saw right through that."

Quinn dropped her hands to her sides. "It comes down to this. She needs us. All of us, especially now. So each of you better find the right words to fix things, or you'll never see your grandchild or her." Quinn pointed at her mother. "Or your niece or nephew." She glared at her sisters. "Cara is six weeks pregnant, so you ladies better fix things, and fix things fast."

Her mom clutched her hand over her heart. "My baby is going to have a baby?" Hope poured from her words, and there was a light in her eyes.

"Oh my God. This should be the happiest time of her life." Becca cupped her face and cried. "We ruined it for her."

"We can make things right." Harper stroked Becca's back. "We will."

"I love her. We all do, and it's time she felt it. Cara is hormonal and having morning sickness, and there aren't enough brownies in all the land to mend her broken heart."

"You just did," Cara said from the doorway as a tear slid down her cheek.

Quinn stood back as the family rushed Cara, each pulling her into a hug and begging for forgiveness as they touched her flat belly. This was better than Quinn could have hoped. She had all of her family in Scotland, and she had a niece or nephew on the way.

Collin entered the room and wrapped his hands around Quinn's belly. "You did good." He kissed her cheek. "Are you going to tell them about ours?"

"Not yet." Quinn patted his hands. "I still have more damage control to do, and then we can truly celebrate." She turned in his arms. "Is everything ready?"

"Aye. You know there's a chance she'll want to kill you."

Quinn shrugged. "It won't be the first time."

Quinn leaned against the Town Car with her sunglasses pulled down over her eyes. Angus remained behind the wheel, sitting in the air conditioner. The plane landed right on time. She spotted Cooper the second he stepped out of the airport. He was tall, dark, handsome, and everything she could ever want for her sister.

"Cooper Cruz?" she asked with arms folded.

"Yeah?" Hearing his name seemed to catch him off guard. "Who are you?"

"Quinn Thatcher." Quinn held out her hand. "I've been expecting you."

"Let me guess, Ian called."

"No, dear," she said, opening the Town Car's back door. "He didn't have to. I sent him."

"Is this another one of the Thorntons' games? Does she know I'm here?"

"No game. The paper I sent was real, although she wasn't the one requesting it. She would have in time." Quinn slid into the car and leaned across the seat, peering up at him. "If you'd rather that day not come, then I suggest you get in."

He slid into the seat. "So it's true that she's pregnant?"

"Aye." Quinn lifted the glass from her head as Cooper shut the door.

"Angus, we're ready."

"She hates me," Cooper announced.

"Hate is a strong word, Mr. Cruz, and my sister uses it sparingly. You're the father of her child. You gave her two

KATE ALLENTON

things in the world that no one else could
ever do."

"Two?"

"The baby and feeling what it's like not
to have a vision when touching someone."
Quinn turned to face him. "If I take you to
see her, I need to know what your
intentions are, because I won't let another
soul hurt her, least of all you."

"Honestly?"

"Honesty is a good start."

"I don't know. I love her. I went crazy
with worry when I couldn't find her. At
first, when Betty told me about her vision,
I didn't want any part of getting to know
Cara. I was headstrong. Being without
her, and worried sick for the last six
weeks, I was scared that I'd never see her
again. And I don't get scared, Quinn. I
don't ever get scared."

Quinn nodded. "Let me make myself
abundantly clear. I have no filter, and I
don't lie. If you hurt my sister again, I will
hunt you down, chop off your dick, and
shove it down your throat." Quinn smiled.
"I'll spend the remainder of my life
thinking of ways to make yours worse. I
can promise that. You think those three
ghosts in your house are bad? Imagine a
hundred. That's my promise to you."

"You're threatening an American
federal agent."

"Good thing we're in Scotland. Now get your head out of your ass, make things right, and don't think about ruining what I have planned."

"Where are we going?" Cooper asked, gazing out the window.

"A special place where the magic happens and dreams can come true."

"You sound like a walking advertisement for Disney."

Quinn smiled. "I can only start the ball rolling. This is it, Cooper Cruz. Make your stand. This is the one and only shot you've got, so don't screw it up."

Cara strolled around the castle on Collin's arm. She'd felt sick to her stomach, and he'd been kind enough to take her for a walk to tour some of the other grounds she'd hadn't yet seen. The fresh air calmed her queasy belly. They'd been to see the horses and everywhere, except where she wanted to go. She'd been dying to see the place where Quinn had first laid eyes on him. The place of the infamous battle and the bridge.

Cara strolled toward the hill that Quinn had named Baby E for Everest. The air in Scotland had mellowed her some. It was as though a switch had been flipped and Quinn was now happy. If only Cara could be.

"This is where she was tackled by Harness."

"The dog?" Cara grinned. "I bet she loved that."

"It ruined her favorite white skirt. She still complains to this day."

Cara chuckled as they entered the empty clearing.

"It was here that Ian and I were sword fighting on horseback. Can you imagine your sister stepping into the fight and whistling to get our attention? Because that's what she did. She proclaimed she had the prize, tossed it at me, and said, 'Game over.' I think it was in that minute that I fell in love with her."

"Now who's fibbing?" Cara squeezed Collin's arm. "We all know why you chased her down. It was because of the curse."

"Aye, the one she told me you saw before you tried to talk her out of coming."

Cara shrugged. "I didn't want to see her hurt."

Collin led her toward a cabin at the end of the clearing and stopped. "You know Quinn loves you."

"Of course," Cara answered. Growing up, she might have questioned it, but not anymore.

"She disna want to see you hurt either. I want you to think about that before you kill her, because kill her, you'll try, and then I'll have to stop the fight. We cannae have your wee one getting hurt, or hers and mine."

"She's pregnant too?"

Collin opened the door and placed his hand on her back, easing her inside before yanking the door closed from the other side. She would have protested, but she stood stunned. Cooper stood in the middle of the small room.

Collin's words made sense now. Her heart raced, heavy in her chest, the beat echoing in her ears. She swallowed the knot that had formed in her throat, and her mouth suddenly ran dry.

"I was going to call you," she whispered. "I just needed more time."

"Six weeks wasn't long enough?" Cooper asked, unmoving from his spot.

"I picked up the phone several times, but I always hung up."

He took a step in her direction and stopped. "Why did you hang up?"

Cara remained silent as she ran through all the reasons in her head. None of them seemed worth the weight they'd carried weeks ago.

"How about I start?" he said as he stepped closer. "I'm sorry I didn't take a chance on you when Betty told me about her vision. I was a skeptic, and when she told me that I'd be the only one not to give you visions, and that we'd one day end up married, I didn't believe. I'm sorry my sister was the center of the danger you went through, and I'm sorry that I broke your trust. But know this, Cara. I'm not sorry I went into your office. I'm not sorry for getting to know you, and I'm damn sure not sorry that you're pregnant."

"You know?" Her brows knit together. "How?"

"It doesn't matter." He closed the distance between them and cupped her cheek. "What matters is that you know I'll never do anything to hurt you again. I love you, Cara, and it about killed me when you disappeared."

Cara lowered her gaze to the floor. She wanted to believe him, more than anything, but after everything she'd been through, she was afraid it was yet another ruse. "If you're saying that because of the baby, Cooper, you don't have to worry. I'll let you in his or her life as much or as little as you want."

Cooper lifted her chin until her gaze to meet his. "You aren't hearing me, Cara. I'll love that baby no matter what, but my life isn't complete without you. I didn't know love until I met you. I didn't realize how much I needed it until you left. Cara...baby. I need you, and I don't need anything else."

Cara chewed her bottom lip. "You once said one problem at a time. I don't want to be a problem, Cooper."

"Don't you get it? You're not a problem. You're my solution, baby. You're more than I could have ever asked for. You're more than I ever dreamed of. Please, baby, give me a second chance to do things right."

Cara nodded, and that was all it took. Coop wrapped her in his arms quicker than she could blink and pressed a kiss to her lips. A spark ignited from that brief touch and settled in her heart, spreading a hazy sense of comfort throughout her body. Relief rolled off him in waves, calming and blanketing her in his warmth.

A second chance was all it took. Within two months, she was married with the last name she'd despised. Within four, Cooper had quit the bureau to help run the bar because he wanted to be there when their child was born. This was her life. It was finally complete. With each visionless touch and each heated kiss, her world was forever rocked by the one man she'd once wasted brownies on.

**I hope you enjoyed Cara's story.
Keep reading for a sneak peek of
Psychic Charm, Harper's story.**

Harper gazed out her office window, the warmth of the sun heating her face. The trees below swayed in a late afternoon breeze. If she closed her eyes, she could almost imagine the smell of the salty air as it drifted from the ocean.

The headset pressed against her ear hummed as the caller spoke. She'd know the caller's voice anywhere; silky, sexy, and dangerous. It vibrated, the voice of the kind of man her momma warned her about and one her Aunt Betty would have tied up in her bed. She was promiscuous like that. A thrill seeker just like Harper.

You don't walk away from his kind. You walk backward and pull him by his tie straight to the bed. It was the reason goose bumps covered her arms, and why she locked her doors at night. For all she knew, the body attached to the voice was short, bald, and would think the big O belonged on the music scale. His voice was probably more than his body could ever deliver. That would be her luck, not that she'd ever invite this guy out for coffee to test her theory. Even she had boundaries, not many, but some.

He hadn't told her exactly what he did, and she'd never asked for fear she'd wind up dead. She was too young to die.

"Harper, are you still there?" His voice oozed sex and wrapped around her body, making her all warm and tingly inside. Whatever his profession, he'd make a killing as a phone sex operator. If she closed her eyes, he could be anyone, anywhere. A stranger on the street, a dark, mysterious man from a bar, her gynecologist. She'd never know until she heard him speak.

The truth was he was just a man on the phone asking her to tap into the energy of a location.

Harper adjusted the headset and moved away from the window. Her gut churned, and yet she couldn't pinpoint why. "I'm still here. Just trying to tap into the energy and get an idea. Where did you say this business trip was taking place?"

"Mexico."

Mexico? Who takes business meetings in Mexico? Drug lords, America's Top 10 Most Wanted hiding from the law, that's who. Not that it was any of her business. She didn't get paid to have an opinion on how this guy ran his life. He paid her for something entirely different; use of her ability to guide him away from danger and uneasy situations. He'd branded her the intuition he'd been born without.

"Mexico," she whispered to herself and closed her eyes. Her gut clenched tight, and her heart pounded frantically. A feeling of unease skittered down her spine. The location wasn't a place she'd soon be visiting. "It doesn't feel right. If I were you, I'd either move it somewhere else or cancel it altogether."

"How about Los Angeles?" He was quick to ask.

Her shoulders immediately relaxed. Her ass cheeks no longer could crack a nut from its shell. That was the place. She felt it in her gut. "That feels a lot better. Relaxing even. Maybe you should extend your stay after the meeting and have a vacation."

His deep laughter filled the line. "You're cute. How much time do we have left?"

His words put a smile on her lips.

"Ten minutes." She ignored the time on the clock. He'd paid for a fifteen-minute psychic call. That was twenty minutes ago. She just couldn't make herself hang up. He was like a drug. A sexy, addictive, in-need-of-rehab drug, and she needed a fix.

"What are you wearing?"

Typical. She'd give him the same answer as last week. He'd asked so many times the question no longer made her blush. "This isn't 1-800-Talk-Dirty-To-Me. I'm wearing clothes."

"You stay dressed a lot."

"People tend to do that when at work."

"Let's play a game. You tell me what you're wearing, and I'll answer one question honestly. Anything you want to know."

"How do I know you're telling your truth?"

"You're psychic."

Harper pressed her lips together. If her sisters knew she was getting personal with a client, well, they'd probably pat her on the back or give her high-fives. They were good like that.

"Fine. I'm wearing a black pencil skirt, a white silk blouse, and three-inch heels."

She totally lied, trying to make herself a more attractive package. Harper ran her sweaty palms down her boyfriend cut jeans she liked to wear loose in case she splurged at lunch and needed the extra room. Jeans that cut into her stomach ranked right up there with an enema.

She glanced down at the coffee stain smack-dab on the lead singer's nose on her favorite concert tee-shirt. She was hopeless.

"Sophisticated, refined, and I bet wearing the heels makes you the perfect height to kiss."

A shrill of excitement traveled down her spine. *Down, girl.*

"Your turn."

"What's your real first name?" The question flew from her mouth before she could stop it. It was the same question she wondered every time he called. Maybe she wanted to know—she had hoped it was Bob or Leroy—to kill some of the fantasy she had after every conversation. *Oh Leroy, take me. That was about as sexy as granny panties.* She needed his name to be like jumping into a bucket of ice.

"That's the question you were waiting to ask? My name?" His voice turned playful. He almost sounded disappointed she hadn't asked how many inches lay behind his zipper.

"It's only fair, you know mine. Don't tell me you're a Harold or a Eugene." *Please do.*

"This is confidential?"

"Like attorney-client privilege. Okay, well, maybe not that. How about, like a barista and a customer. What's the name they put on your cup?" She'd bet he ordered his extra hot and black.

"Ryker Cage."

"Of course it is." Her hand flew to cover her mouth, and her eyes bulged. She couldn't believe she'd just blurted that out loud.

A low, throaty, very masculine chuckle reached her ears, making her goosebumps add an extra layer. "My turn. What's your favorite dessert?"

"Anything chocolate," she answered without hesitation. "You?"

"The chocolate left on your lips."

She fanned herself, trying to control the heat flooding her body. Blood rushed to her cheeks, and she bit her lip to keep from moaning. This guy was good. Too good. "Okay, I think your time's up."

"Harper." The way he said her name left her breathless.

"Yeah?"

"My time was up thirty minutes ago. We'll talk again soon. You can count on it, princess."

A dial tone filled her ears, and she let out the breath she'd been holding, yanked the headset from her ears, and tossed it onto her desk. What was it with that man? Every time he called, she felt like she'd run a marathon. A sexy, naked, in-the-mud marathon, but a marathon nonetheless. The first time he'd called, he'd asked to speak to a manager, and he'd been asking for her ever since.

Harper's assistant, Patricia, peeked into the office before walking in with a folder and a package that she so politely laid in the inbox. Harper's eyes narrowed as she regarded the extra work. Her day was getting longer by the minute as a headache attempted to form at her temples. She bet Ryker knew a good cure for getting rid of headaches. She shoved the thought aside. The folder, the package. She should be thankful for a distraction.

"Is that time sensitive?"

"Would I have brought it in if it wasn't?" Patricia smiled and parked her butt in one of the office chairs. It was her not-so-subtle way to hurry Harper along.

Picking up the folder, Harper flipped it open. The small print on the contract made her eyes cross. "Give me Cliff Notes."

"It's a contract for the new security and IT guy that you finally got your sisters to agree to. He's rewiring the entire building with new stuff for better performance and security."

"Who picked this guy?"

"Quinn, I believe."

Harper flipped to the money amount and what was involved. "Anything in the contract out of the ordinary? Any clauses that agrees to the equivalent of kicking a puppy?"

Patricia smiled. "No. I read it. It's a standard contract. One-year term with the cost of monitoring and system upgrades. Nothing strange."

"Will he need to bring the call center down?"

"Afraid so." She pressed her lips together and cringed as if waiting for her bark.

Harper hated to take the company offline. It had been the main reason her sisters always opposed the upgrade, but it really needed to be done. They had a ton of confidential files rotting in the basement that needed to be uploaded into something secure. "Do we really need to take down the entire system?"

"The death threats from the crazies and religious fanatics that want to burn the building have doubled. I think it's a smart move to get it all done at once."

Harper nodded and scribbled her signature at the bottom before handing it back.

"Coordinate a shutdown the week before Christmas and send out an email to the staff and post an announcement on our website for our clients."

Patricia's fingers flew over the keyboard on her phone as if she'd been expecting Harper's request. She'd probably seen it coming. She was gifted too.

"What's in the package?"

She shrugged. "Not sure. A courier dropped it off about fifteen minutes ago. There's no return address, just your name."

Harper lifted the package to her ear and closed her eyes. No ticking. "Thanks."

Patricia rose and headed for the door.

"Hey, Patricia. Is Grace still in the office?"

Patricia turned, walking backward.

"No, Grace was meeting your mother and your Aunt Betty."

Better Grace than Harper. Their mom was a handful all by herself. Throw crazy Aunt Betty, who owned the Thin Blue Line police bar, into the mix, and there was no telling what Grace was having to deal with or how much she would have to spend on bail.

Harper nodded and returned her attention to the brown package in non-descript wrapping. Her name was scribbled on the top in a masculine handwriting. She closed her eyes and sensed the package. It was the same energy that cocooned her when she spoke to Ryker; all consuming. Interesting.

She ripped into the brown packing and tossed it into her garbage. A blue box sat inside. It was the kind that women fantasize about from the store where everything was overpriced and shiny.

A card was attached to the delicate white bow.

Harper sat back in the chair and stared at it as if it was a new species yet discovered. *He's lost his ever-lovin' mind.*

She could read the card and make sure. Yeah, she could at least read the card.

She ran her finger under the flap and slid the card out.

*I have your direct line. I thought it was time
that you had mine.
~R*

Ryker. His name popped instantly into her mind. How had he known she would ask his name, even if he'd planned to play the game? Maybe he hadn't.

Screw it. Harper eased the lid on the box open, gently pulled back the white tissue paper, and grinned. A can of mace sat next to a phone identical to the one nestled inside her purse. The screen was turned on. The screen saver had the word "Princess."

She picked it out of the box and pressed a button to make the phone come to life. A notification said there was an unread text message. She should have put the phone back. She should have walked away. She should have done a million things. What she shouldn't have done was actually open the message to see what it said.

*Princess,
It's time we meet.
Ryker*

"Oh, I don't think so, buddy." Who does that?

The phone in her hands rang, making her jump. The caller ID read Ryker. Her finger hovered over the decline button. At the last minute, she answered the call and pressed the phone to her ear.

"This is borderline stalking," she blurted out before he could speak.

"I knew you'd be cautious, but I also know you're curious, so I'll make this easy for you. Regardless if you agree to meet me, I've programmed my number into this phone. If you ever need me, just call or text."

"Why would I—"

"If you'd like to meet, LeRochelle at seven. It's public and has security. You can bring the mace. Nothing will happen to you there. Not that I'd ever do anything to harm you."

"You're crazy." And so was she for even considering it. She should have hung up and tossed the phone, but there was something about Ryker that made her keep listening.

"I've been called worse."

"Didn't your momma ever warn you about stranger danger? I could be some deranged psycho chick and you....well, you could be my boring accountant. I'd hate to have to stab your eyes with the toothpick from a fruity drink."

His chuckle filled the line and eased her tension. He had a unique sense of stifling her unease and, what was odd, calming people. That was one of her specialties. "I'm not worried."

"Ryker. How about we keep things professional, and I forget you ever sent this...phone."

"You could, or you could finally at least have a face to put with my voice. One drink. If I'm inappropriate, you get up and leave. If I scare you, spray me with mace and then get up and leave. If I turn out to be the accountant, poke my eyes out and then leave. I won't even put up a fight."

Harper chewed her bottom lip and clenched her eyes closed as she searched for the energy in his words and the location. Nothing. She was nuts for even considering it.

"My momma is gonna be mad if you make me a statistic. I can see it now. My story will be used in an updated training video on what *not* to do when taking calls." She clutched the phone tighter in her hand. "If I'm going to do this, then I pick the place."

"Where did you have in mind?"

"The Thin Blue Line beach bar." An off-the-wall outlandish location, but a scream in that bar would cut the cop response time to mere seconds, killing the need to write out her obituary before having to leave work. No way was she leaving that job up to her sisters. They'd paint her as a boring spinster cat lady. She was allergic to cats. No obit for her, not with cops within arm's reach. Did they carry guns into bars? She was about to find out.

"The cop hang-out?"

"Take it or leave it, Ryker Cage."

"You're a smart woman taking precaution. I'll meet you on the back deck at seven."

"You got a thing against a crowd of cops?"

"Let's just say, in my line of work, I stay off the radar."

What the hell did he do? A hit man? A mobster? Did Florida even have a mob? Oh God, was he in a gang? And why was he even in town? Warning bells triggered in her mind. Why would she even think this was a good idea?

"Wait, Ryker, I..." The line disconnected, and the phone went blank. She shrugged and tossed the phone into her purse, along with the note and the pepper spray.

"Smart, Harper," she chided herself. "I wasn't only getting personal information from a client over the phone. In two hours, I'd know his face." She should be kicking her ass when, in reality, she was already three steps ahead, running a mental inventory of her closet in her head. What did one wear when meeting Mr-Sexy-Voice-Potential-Killer-Mob-Boss? Shoes for a quick exit or shoes to impress?

Harper picked up her phone and dialed Patricia's extension. "I need coffee and lots of it."

"Sure."

Harper hung the phone up. She had some digging to do. If she was even thinking about meeting up with the stranger, she'd know everything about him before she left. Twisting her hair up into a bun, she slid her pen through the strands to hold it in place and devoted the next three hours into decoding exactly who was Ryker Cage.

Harper's story is available for preorder and is scheduled for release on 11/14/16.

Once again, thank you for reading my books. I appreciate each and every one of you.

Text KATE to 313131 and get a text message on release dates!

Sign up for her newsletters at
www.kateallenton.com

Other Books by Kate Allenton

Suggested Reading Order

BENNETT SISTERS BOX SET (Books 1-4 in one bundle, 1218 pages)

INTUITION (Book 1)

TOUCH OF FATE (Book 2)

MIND PLAY (Book 3)

THE RECKONING (Book 4)

REDEMPTION (Book 5)

CHANCE ENCOUNTERS (Book 6)

DESTINED HEARTS (Book 7)

PHANTOM PROTECTORS BOX SET (Books 1-4 in one bundle, 964 pages)

RECKLESS ABANDON (Book 1)

BETRAYAL (Book 2)

UNTAMED (Book 3)

GUIDED LOYALTY (Book 4)

CARRINGTON-HILL INVESTIGATIONS

DECEPTION (Book 1)

DEADLY DESIRE (Book 2)

SHIFTER PARADISE BOX SET

NOT MY SHIFTER/ SINFULLY CURSED

KARMA

SOPHIE MASTERSON SERIES/ DIXON SECURITY

LIFTING THE VEIL (Book 1)

BEYOND THE VEIL (Book 2)

VEILED INTENTIONS (Book 3)

VEILED THREATS (Book 4)

THE LOVE FAMILY SERIES

SKYLAR (BOOK1)

DECLAN (BOOK 2)

FLYNN (BOOK 3)

REED (BOOK 4)

LANDON (BOOK 5)

ALEXIS (BOOK 6)

GABE (BOOK 7)

JACKSON (BOOK 8)

LINKED INC.

DEADLY INTENT (BOOK 1)

PSYCHIC LINK (BOOK 2)

PSYCHIC CHARM (BOOK 3)

HELL BOUND

MYSTIC TIDES BOX SET

About the Author

Kate has lived in Florida for most of her entire life. She enjoys a quiet life with her husband, Michael and two kids.

Kate has pulled all-nighters finishing her favorite books and also writing them. She says she'll sleep when she's dead or when her muse stops singing off key.

She loves creating worlds full of suspense, secrets, hunky men, kick ass heroines, steamy sex and oh yeah the love of a lifetime. Not to mention an occasional ghost and other supernatural talents thrown into the mix.

She loves to hear from her readers by email at KateAllenton@hotmail.com, on Twitter@KateAllenton, and on Facebook at facebook.com/kateallenton.1

Visit her website at www.kateallenton.com

Visit Coastal Escape Publishing's website at www.coastalescapepublishing.com

www.ingramcontent.com/pod-product-compliance
Lightning Source LLC
Chambersburg PA
CBHW071908220626
47052CB00002B/267